Serpent's Keep 3
The Outland

David R. Beshears

Large Print Edition

Greybeard Publishing
Washington State

Greybeard Publishing
P.O. Box 480
McCleary, WA 98557-0480

ISBN 978-1-947231-25-2
(large print edition)

Serpent's Keep 3

The Outland

Chapter One

The gently rolling landscape of the northeastern Outland was a blanket of fir and alder, the forest canopy unbroken but for the occasional grassy meadow or small lake, the occasional spire of one or another of the six temples that were poking up through the trees. The setting sun's multi-colored rays streaked through the upper branches of the green canopy with very little managing to reach the forest floor below.

Jake and Meara had found their way to an isolated clearing a hundred feet or so off the main trail. They had cleared away the thick mulch from the center of the clearing and the flickering light of a campfire pushed the shadows of dusk into the surrounding trees and undergrowth.

Jake was sitting near the fire. A bloodied, hastily applied bandage was wrapped around his left forearm. Meara, one of her hands also wrapped in a bandage, her cheek swollen and showing the early signs of bruising, was cleaning an open wound on Jake's temple. She rummaged around in a gray canvas bag and brought out a small plastic vial. She opened it, dabbed some of its contents onto a square cloth and applied it to Jake's head wound. Jake stiffened but managed to hold his silence.

Jacob Quigley was now in his early twenties, but something in the eyes reflected the life experiences of someone much older. Meara, just coming out of her teens herself, carried the wisdom of someone well beyond her years.

Just at the moment though, none of that seemed to matter for either of them.

Meara finished the first aid work on Jake's head wound and turned her attention to his arm. She carefully unbound the temporary bandage, exposing a three inch long gash, half an inch wide, dark and bleeding.

"Gruesome, but clean," she said. She brought a bottle out of the first aid bag, opened it and poured the clear liquid liberally into the wound.

"Oh boy…" said Jake, hissing through clenched teeth.

Meara grumbled out a low *yup* as she worked. She squeezed the gash closed with one hand as she tightly wrapped the arm with a clean bandage. Finished then, she began tossing the dirty bandages into the fire.

"Thanks," said Jake. He looked about their surroundings. "Waddya figure, Meara? Two days from the village?"

"Yes sir. About that. Maybe three." Meara put the first aid supplies back into the bag. She sat back then and looked up at the darkening sky. "Best we stay here tonight, start out at dawn."

Jake gave a nod in answer. He shifted about and faced the small fire. The forest around them was quiet ahead of the night, the encroaching shadows of dusk growing quickly darker.

"That shouldn't be a problem," he said then, almost to himself.

"Yes sir," said Meara. "We weren't followed."

"No, I expect not."

There had been just three bandits, and two of them had suffered injuries much more severe than they had dealt to Jake and Meara. The third had run off with minor wounds. Jake guessed the three were what had constituted one of the lesser bands and were not part of either of the two main bandit groups that roamed the Outland. Neither of these two larger bands was thought to be currently in this part of the Outland.

There was the wolf pack however, a large group of *smart wolves* that roamed a wide range of the Outland, coming and going at will from some unknown location. Worse yet, its leader had a particular grievance against Jake and Meara.

Jake indicated Meara's bandaged hand.

"How's the hand?" he asked.

Meara absently worked the fingers. "Fine, sir."

"Good..." He pointed then to Meara's discolored cheek. "That's gonna bruise."

Meara shrugged and said nothing.

Jake looked about them again.

"I'll fix us something to eat," he said. "You stand watch."

"Yes sir." She considered then. "Sir?"

"Yeah?" Jake was reaching for his backpack.

"One of the temples." Meara indicated west. "It's maybe half a day from here."

Jake brought a bag of rations out of his pack, dug around again for the deep metal dish. He looked then from Meara to the west.

"That might not be a bad idea," he said noncommittally.

"Yes sir." Meara clambered slowly to her feet, using her staff for support. "I'll give the perimeter a check."

The southland temple, unlike the temple near the village of Serpent's Keep, had changed little since its original construction, with just a few additions completed over the many years. There was the main building, the two short wings and a handful of separate outbuildings. A pair of spires rose high above the sanctuary, poking above the canopy of the surrounding forest. A knee-high wall ran the perimeter of the roof of the central structure.

Master Peter stepped out of the temple's primary meeting room, crossed the foyer and started into the main hallway of the east wing. He entered the dining hall.

Only two of the tables were occupied, despite this being midday. He walked across the room to the serving table, picked up a bowl of stew and a spoon, and sat at the nearest empty table.

Peter was in his early sixties, though he could pass for someone much younger. He was dressed in the traditional heavy brown robe of his temple, bound at the waist with a tan cloth belt. His dark brown hair, curling around his ears, was in a constant state of disarray.

His meeting with the head staff of this temple had gone well. Peter had gotten along very well with the abbot and they had felt as brothers from their first meeting, despite their two temples having long been separated. They spoke of the work of their two sanctuaries, the ancient history of the six temples, and what role the temples might play in the recently reintegrated Outland.

Master Peter intended the brothers of the temples to take on a leadership role in the Outland.

The two temples had already worked together to reestablish a presence at another temple in another segment of the Outland, this one long abandoned. No decision had yet been made regarding yet another, distant sanctuary that was now occupied by Janice and the Rhetani.

As for the other two temples, no one had yet reached the distant temple known to exist far to the north; the sixth temple, a ruin now little more than jagged shards of broken walls, had been visited only once and was not thought to be recoverable.

Brother John entered the dining hall with Master Edmund, the temple abbot. Edmund gave a nod to Peter before walking over to one of the occupied tables that he might talk with his monks. John collected a food bowl from the serving table and sat at the table with Peter. He considered the gray contents of his bowl, stirring it with his spoon.

"Believe me when I say that I am most grateful for their hospitality, Master Peter," he said quietly. "That being said, I am all the more appreciative of the bounty of our own sanctuary."

"We are indeed blessed, John," said Peter. He swallowed a spoonful of his stew. "Still, it is not so bad."

John lifted a spoonful from his bowl, let the contents settle in his mouth for a moment. He swallowed, tried a charitable smile. He was only partially successful.

"What next, sir?" he asked.

"Home I believe, where we shall prepare for a journey north."

"To the North Temple then," said John.

The monks had developed or reestablished an extensive network of trails throughout much of the Outland over the past few months, but there were no known trails in the far north. They would be trailblazing much of their journey to the North Temple.

"It should prove to be most interesting," said Peter. "No doubt quite the experience."

"Yes sir," said John.

Master Edmund finished his conversation with the two monks at the other table, stepped across the room and stood before Peter and Brother John. He clasped his hands before him and gave a broad smile.

"And how is the stew today, brothers?" he asked.

"Just fine, Master Edmund," said John. "Thank you."

Peter gave a quick glance and smile to John, again to Edmund. "The generosity of your temple is very much appreciated."

"Yes," John said quickly. "Much appreciated."

"Our pleasure, to be sure." Edmund nodded in welcome. Prior to the reintegration of the Outland, visitors to his sanctuary had been almost unheard of.

"Brother John was just commenting on your hospitality," said Peter.

"You are very kind, Brother John," said Edmund, smiling even more broadly.

A young, small-statured monk stepped into the doorway and looked about the dining hall. Seeing Edmund, he moved quickly across to the table. He stood silent beside Edmund and waited to be acknowledged.

"Yes, Brother Gerald?" prompted Edmund.

"So sorry to bother you, Master Edmund," said Gerald. "We have just received word. Brothers Jasper and Hugh... they are bringing Jacob Quigley and his associate in."

"Pardon?" said Peter, setting his spoon beside his half-empty bowl.

"Yes, Master Peter." Young Gerald wasn't sure whom to address. He decided on his own abbot. "They suffered some injuries, I understand. Attacked by bandits, I understand."

"Thank you, Gerald," said Edmund. He turned to his guests as everyone stood. "Shall we go to meet them?"

Peter and John followed Edmund out of the dining room and down the hall to the front foyer. Stepping through the heavy front doors, Peter moved across the porch to stand at the top of the steps. Only moments later Jake and Meara came into view in the clearing below; several monks were walking beside them, ready to assist if needed. Brother John stepped past Peter and quickly descended the steps to help.

Master Edmund stood beside Peter.

"Walking wounded, it would appear," he said.

"It would take more than a bandit attack to bring down those two," said Peter.

"So it would seem."

Sheriff Smith stood in front of the café, having just finished an early lunch. He looked up and down the wide, cobblestone street that was the main thoroughfare of the village. He was in his late forties, tall with broad shoulders. He was dressed in light brown slacks and a long-sleeved button shirt; a simple badge pinned above his left shirt pocket identified him as sheriff.

He had been sheriff for much of his adult life and it showed in the calm, confident way that he carried himself. He was quite comfortable in his role as the sheriff of Serpent's Keep.

He stepped away from the café and started down the street. The buildings to either side were mostly single storey, with only an occasional two-storey structure. At first glance, the village looked like something out of the distant past, but closer examination showed a curious mix of eras. The street lamps lining the thoroughfare were both gas and electric. The buildings were rustic but clean, made of stone, wood, brick or adobe. The windows had glass panes set into wood frames. Doors rested on heavy hinges and had heavy latches.

Very little had changed in the village since the reintegration of the surrounding Outland several months earlier; this, even with the increased isolation from the outside world.

Sheriff Smith started across the street. He stopped when Mrs. Hodges called out to him.

"Mrs. Hodges," he said, giving a nod hello. "How are you today?"

"Just fine, Sheriff. And you?"

"I am fine indeed, ma'am."

He turned then and the two of them started walking, Mrs. Hodges pulling her two-wheeled wire cart along behind her. She was evidently returning from the market plaza.

Mrs. Hodges was in her sixties, medium height, with strong facial features and sharp eyes. Her medium-brown hair was streaked with gray, was long but kept pulled back. She had run the housekeeping and the kitchen at the Quigley Estate for as long as Sheriff Smith could remember, at least as long as he had been the village sheriff and for years before that. She had changed hardly at all in all those years, was as alive and as spry and healthy as ever.

"How go things at the mansion, Mrs. Hodges?" he asked.

"All is quiet for the moment, Sheriff," she said. "Master Quigley and young Jacob are both away just now."

"So I was given to understand."

"Yes. It is just me and Mr. Griffin, and Mr. Griffin is often mistaken for being absent, the way the man blends into the woodwork."

Sheriff Smith smiled. "I have often had that impression of the man."

They walked in silence for a few paces, then stopped as they reached the door of the sheriff's office. Mrs. Hodges pulled the cart up close and stood it on end.

"I have been meaning to drop in to see you, Sheriff," she said. "A question, if I may."

"Of course, ma'am. What is it?"

"Well, sir," she started. "To now, the Outland was the Outland and the Village was the Village. I have never felt, not in all my years, I have never felt the Outland might be encroaching on Serpent's Keep. All the dangers were on the other side of village wall. Within these walls, we were safe."

"I would consider that a reasonable assumption, Mrs. Hodges." The sheriff thought on that for a moment. "Ma'am, I understand your unease. Indeed, much out there has changed. The Outland is now a very different place. But I can assure you, we recognize that we are in a new world. We have adapted as necessary."

The sheriff had worked with the Captain of the Watch to enhance the security at each of the village gates. Two person teams now walked outside the village wall. Small teams periodically went into the Outland, walked the north road to the Farm and the west trail to the nearby temple. The Farm now had fulltime security.

All of this meant that the village residents rotated duty through the civilian guard much more quickly.

"Is there something specific that concerns you?" he asked.

"Not directly," she admitted. But there were those who visited her back-alley booth seeking special preparations to take with them into the Outland. They came to her with stories, and with fears of what they might next face in the Outland.

There were new dangers out there.

"No," she said then. "I suppose not. Not directly."

Sheriff Smith put on his most supportive, assuring expression; well-practiced, in times like these.

"Do not worry, Mrs. Hodges," he said. "What needs to be done is being done."

"No doubt," she sighed.

"Please, don't hesitate to come to me with your concerns. You no doubt hear from folks who are not likely to come to me."

"I'll do that," said Mrs. Hodges. She shifted her wire cart around, prepared to leave. "I should go."

"It was good to see you," said the sheriff. "And please, Mrs. Hodges. Don't worry. We're ready for whatever might come our way."

"Yes. I'm sure you are right. Thank you, Sheriff."

The sheriff watched Mrs. Hodges continue down the thoroughfare, pulling her cart along behind her. He took out his key then, took the final step up to the door of his office. He unlocked the door and went inside.

It was a small room, furnished with a desk, a filing cabinet and a couple of chairs. Another door led to a short hall with bathroom, storage closet and several cells.

Smith went to the small table in one corner behind his desk. He picked up the coffee pot, flipped the lid and held the pot to his nose: it smelled old but drinkable. He poured the last of the coffee into a ceramic mug, turned back to his desk and sat down, the chair screeching painfully. He was just pulling himself forward when the door opened and Mason came into his office.

Sheriff Smith leaned back, to another squeal from the chair, and brought the cup to his lips. He took a long swallow as he watched Mason close the door and step fully into the room.

Mason placed a hand on the back of the guest chair and looked across the desk to the sheriff.

"Sheriff Smith," he stated.

"Hello, Mason. What can I do for you?" The sheriff took another sip from his coffee. He stared into his cup, gave a grimace.

Okay, not as drinkable as he had first thought...

He indicated the guest chair. Mason considered, finally stepped around the chair and sat down.

"Sheriff Smith," he said again.

"Mason." Smith sat forward, eyes on Mason as he absently set the cup down. "Is there a problem?"

Most of the citizenry considered Mason to be the village eccentric, and his actions and pronouncements did little to dissuade them of that belief. But the man's observations often turned out to be dead on. He took careful handling, and took a disproportionate amount of the sheriff's time, but Smith never dismissed Mason out of hand.

"A problem, sir?" Mason responded sharply. "The outside world that was once known to be out there is lost to us. We are wholly alone."

"That's not really news, Mason," said Smith. This was an earlier observation of Mason's that had proven true. There had been no contact with the outside world for a long time, since well before the bizarre changes to the Outland. The Outland, in which the village of Serpent's Keep existed, was now a world unto itself.

"And yet you sit there as if nothing has changed," said Mason.

There must be something in the air...

Sheriff Smith pushed his cup aside. He would need to make a fresh pot. "Our interactions with the outside were always infrequent, and you yourself have argued more than once that what little contact there was with the outside was never good for us."

"Not the point. Not the point."

"Okay," said Smith. "And the point would be…"

Mason leaned forward, slid forward in the chair. He placed his forearms on the sheriff's desk.

"Our isolation is not our vulnerability, sir."

"It isn't…" Smith said flatly.

"No sir. It is not. It is rather the false sense that all that can be seen can be controlled."

"Excuse me?" Smith prompted. Getting Mason to get to the point was often a chore.

"There are those, those out there in this new, greater Outland, who see what has happened as their opportunity to step in and impose their will, their philosophy, upon us all, upon this world with very real borders."

"All right, Mason," said Smith. *Yes. There is definitely something in the air.* He leaned back in his chair to its accompanying squeal. "What do you suggest we do about that?"

"We need to send out another team," said Mason, sliding his forearms further onto the desk.

"You mean the Road?" A team had been sent out weeks before to verify that the outside world was no longer there. They had followed the road that led from the village front gate to the outside world beyond; the real world.

What they found was that the Outland was indeed alone.

"The Road," said Mason. "Yes."

"Mason, you know better than I that there is no longer a world beyond our own. There is nothing out there."

Wow, thought Sheriff Smith. *To say that out loud...*

Mason gave a sharp nod. "I have just said as much."

"Mason." Sheriff Smith rubbed at his temple. "What do you want?"

"I want to know what has *replaced* the outside world."

"Excuse me? You want what?"

Mason slid back from the desk and let his arms drop into his lap.

"There is *something* out there," he said. "There is something beyond our world, out there, where the outside world used to be. If we are to stand against those who would dominate the Outland, dominate us, we must seek an ally."

"An ally," Sheriff Smith said in a sigh. "Assuming there is actually something out there, something that the last team did not find, I would hasten to add, what makes you think that this *something* would be our ally?"

"Will they?" said Mason. "I do not know. Let's find them. Let's ask them."

Sheriff Smith let that last settle in. He leaned further back in his chair, studied the odd little man sitting on the other side of the desk. Mason, in turn, sat silent, waiting for the sheriff to come to a decision and get things going.

Smith sat forward and turned about in his chair.

"I'm going to make some fresh coffee," he said. "You want some?"

Chapter Two

Jake folded his blanket and set it at the foot of the cot. He sat down then and pulled on his hiking boots and started lacing them up. Filtered sunlight streamed in from the small, narrow window behind him and onto the floor of the sleeping cell, the only light in the room.

Dressed then, he pushed his backpack under the cot and left the cell. The hallway was similar to those that he had found in all the temples. Widely-placed oil lamp sconces were mounted on the walls, their dull light managing to push back the dark just enough that Jake could see where he was going.

He found Meara in the dining room, sitting alone with a bowl of oatmeal.

Jake collected a bowl for himself and sat at the table opposite her.

"Good morning," he said.

"Sir." Meara kept eating her breakfast.

Jake glanced about them. Three monks were in the room, each sitting alone at their own tables.

Monks were monks, no matter the temple; usually up well before dawn, an early breakfast, and off then to their duties. Being this late in the morning, these three probably worked some odd shift or had just returned to the temple from some outside errand or other.

Jake looked over his spoon to Meara. The bruise on her cheek had had enough time to begin showing its colors; a mix of dark purple and midnight blue.

"Does it hurt?" he asked.

"Sir?"

He pointed with his spoon. "The bruise. Kinda ugly."

"It's fine, sir. It only hurts when I'm reminded of it."

"Right. Gotcha."

For a few long moments they each focused on their breakfast, spooning oatmeal.

"You?" she asked then. She indicated the wounds at his temple and on his arm, both freshly cleaned and treated by the monks.

"Oh, I expect I'll live," said Jake, shrugging. Unseen were the bruised ribs, which were tightly bound beneath his shirt.

"That's good, sir."

"That it is," Jake said calmly; another spoon of oatmeal.

They ate in silence for several minutes. They were just finishing their breakfast when Master Peter entered the dining hall. He looked quickly about the room before stepping over to Jake and Meara's table.

"And how are you two feeling this morning?" he asked.

"Well enough, Brother Peter." Jake indicated a chair.

Peter pulled out the chair and sat down.

"Well enough to travel?"

"We'll be heading home in a few days," said Jake.

"Good, good," said Peter. "I'm sure you can take whatever time you need."

"They've made us feel very welcome."

"To be sure. Master Edmund has been most gracious to us as well," said Peter. "Listen, should you feel up to it, we will be starting out for home tomorrow. You are certainly welcome to join us. Again, should you feel up to it."

Jake looked across the table to Meara. "Waddya say, Meara? You feel up to it?"

"Safety in numbers, sir," she said in answer.

"My thoughts exactly," said Peter. As precarious and downright unsafe as the Outland had been in the past, it was more so now; dangers familiar and known, dangers new and as yet undiscovered.

This, young Jacob and his companion knew all too well.

"All right, then," said Jake. Turning to Peter, "I guess we feel up to it."

"Very good," said Peter. He slid his chair back and stood up. "There is much yet to do this morning. I will see you two later."

"Yes, Master Peter," said Meara.

"Until then," said Jake.

Peter took several steps toward the door, came to an easy stop and looked back.

"Ah. Jacob. I meant to ask..."

Jake was gathering up their bowls and spoons. He stacked them and looked to Peter. "Yes?"

"Has there been any word of Brother Tobias?"

"We left the village a couple of days after he went out," said Jake. "We've been out of touch since."

"Too bad, too bad," said Peter.

"Sorry."

"No. Not at all." Peter gave a smile, turned again and left the dining hall.

Tobias Quigley finished filling his canteen, screwed on the cap and got back to his feet. He looked up and down the creek as he slipped the canteen into the holster on his hip. He picked up his backpack, slid his arms into the shoulder straps, clipped the belt and started out again.

He had been working his way deeper into the Great Ravine since early morning. If a portal yet remained to reach any of the Jahai communities, which had been closed to the Outland since its reintegration, it would be in the Great Ravine. Tobias had nonetheless taken the long way around to get there, wanting to touch base with the handful of side passage access points that had once existed in each of the long-segregated Outland landscapes.

The gateways existing in the primary Outland had long ago been closed off, this back when Tobias' nephew Jacob had restored Serpent's Gate. Unknown to Tobias until later, though, was that a few side threads had remained.

Now... following the reintegration of the Outland itself and the secondary closure of the web, if any threads remained out there, doubtful really, they would be isolated and nearly impossible to find.

Tobias came to a stop. He dropped slowly to one knee in a smooth, easy motion and went perfectly still.

Up ahead, in the distance...

A shadow had moved across the trail ahead, gliding through the mote-filled stream of sunlight that reached through the canopy and down to the forest floor.

He watched and waited, studying the shadows.

There. Again. Nearer now.

A dark silhouette moved out of and back into the darker shadows in the trees.

Tobias brought his knife out from its boot sheath. He didn't expect bandits in the Great Ravine, but best be ready.

A lone Bentai Jahai stepped into the small clearing ahead, some twenty feet in front of Tobias. He stopped, paused, watching Tobias for reaction.

The Bentai were much more humanoid in physical appearance than other Jahai species, and this one managed an almost human stance, despite its dragon-like features.

Tobias slowly stood, returning his knife into its sheath. He smiled, gave a formal nod.

He recognized this Jahai.

"Khol," he said. "My friend."

Khol nodded formally in return. He was about a head taller than Tobias, with sloping shoulders, a large head and a protruding snout. He had extraordinarily long fingers ending in curved black claws. He was dressed in an open leather vest and a calf-length skirt.

"Dear friend Tobias Quigley," he said.

"Do you travel alone, my friend?" asked Tobias.

"Most sadly, yes."

Khol served at the side of Natan, the leader of the Jahai. He would not be apart from Natan of his own choosing.

"I am sorry to hear that," said Tobias. He moved nearer Khol, who also stepped closer. "You were separated from the Jahai Village then."

The Jahai Village, known to most non-Jahai as the Village of the Dragons, was the administrative capital of the Jahai outside of the Jahai home worlds. It was the site of the Grand Hall and the home of Natan.

"I was." Khol was quite despondent. "I was away from the Village when the event occurred, the dissolution of the web. I was left behind."

"And you now seek a thread."

"I have found none to now, neither to return home nor anywhere else."

"I too search for a way to reach your brethren," said Tobias. "We can seek a thread together, if you wish."

Khol tilted his head. He pushed his snout forward.

"I would like that, Tobias Quigley," he said.

"Very well, friend Khol." Tobias started forward, allowing Khol to follow beside him. "Let us talk of our separate travels to now as we walk."

Tobias and Khol continued further into the Great Ravine together.

Janice reached the trailhead and stepped into the wide clearing that was spread before the temple the Rhetani had taken possession of. Martin followed, stepping up beside her. Both carried light packs on their backs, wore utility belts with canteens and sheathed knives strapped to their hips.

They had been gone three days. It felt good to be home.

Janice was a well-kept middle-aged woman, with a smooth complexion but for the slightest onset of wrinkles at the corners of her sharp blue eyes. Her brown hair, unchanged for years, was full, falling to her shoulders.

Martin, in his late thirties, was a short, squat man with disheveled hair and ill-fitting clothes. He had been Janice's assistant for several years, though it seemed much longer to him.

"That is surely a sight for sore eyes," he said, admiring the rundown temple.

"So they say." Janice shifted her backpack and started across the clearing toward the front steps.

The temple was very much as the others, with but a few additions since its original construction. It had been abandoned at some point after the division of the Outland, and had been empty at the time Janice and Martin had found it. They had settled in well before the Outland's recent reintegration, and it was now the official headquarters of the Rhetani, at least so far as Janice was concerned. They had no way of knowing if there were any of the Rhetani high council remaining; if there were, there was no way of contacting them, no way to reach them.

A few Rhetani stragglers, finding themselves isolated from the outside world and alone in this reintegrated Outland, had managed to find their way to the temple over these past months. And so Janice was slowly rebuilding the Rhetani.

She reached the top step as the heavy double doors of the temple opened and Thomas stepped out.

"Janice," he said. "It is good to see you safely home."

Thomas was a few years older than Janice. He was tall, thin, his short hair beginning to gray. His clothes, while old and thread-bare, were clean and neat, as was the man himself.

"Thank you, Thomas." She slipped out of her backpack and handed it to Martin. "Thank you, Martin."

Martin took the backpack, gave a nod to Janice; a nod then to Thomas as he stepped past him and went into the sanctuary.

Janice turned around and looked out across the clearing and to the surrounding forest beyond.

"Have the security issues been taken care of?" she asked. Janice had grown increasingly concerned with the temple defenses. There had as yet been no indication that any of the bandit bands had reached this part of the Outland, but she was certain that it was only a matter of time.

"Yes, ma'am," said Thomas. "Most of the required measures have been implemented, the remaining soon will be."

Janice gave a curt nod in response. There were as yet only a handful of Rhetani living at the temple, so they had had to get creative with the security measures. She had noted on her way in the clearing away of the surrounding brush, though she had not seen the alert trip wires and other perimeter measures.

Barely visible had been the guard on watch up on the roof. Even with all members included in the guard rotation, with so few Rhetani most would be pulling a three hour shift every two to three days.

She would review the security measures being implemented within the temple itself later.

Thomas realized that Janice would not be responding further. He cleared his throat.

"Ma'am," he prompted. "Your trip. Was it successful?"

With each journey out, Janice and Martin pushed the boundaries of their territory, searching for resources the temple might be able to use, looking for anyone living nearby, whether they be potential allies or possible threats.

And they sought other Rhetani, stragglers left behind in one or another of the long-separated Outland segments at the time they had been brought back together.

"Martin has the list," she said. Martin mapped their travels as they went, marking the locations where they had identified resources to be brought back to the temple.

"I'll detail a team," said Thomas.

Janice gave another curt nod, acknowledging Thomas' statement. She turned to him then, contemplated for a moment, again looked outward.

"Thomas," she began.

"Ma'am?"

"I believe we should consider an alliance, of a sort, with one of the bandit bands."

"Janice, I—"

"I understand your concern," she said quickly, cutting him off. "Believe me, I do. Any such association would be limited in scope and the parties would maintain both distance and autonomy."

"To what end, if I might ask?"

"Of course, Thomas." Janice grew thoughtful. "Such would serve two purposes, I should think. First, we are as yet too few in number to push ahead on our plans regarding the Outland populace."

"True enough," Thomas said, reluctantly.

"And with an alliance, the bandits are less likely to mount an assault on our little sanctuary."

The bandits may not be an immediate threat, thought Janice, *but it is only a matter of time...*

"With all due respect, of that I am not so sure."

"You think not?"

"I believe they are just the sort to bite the hand that feeds them." Thomas gave a gentle nod. "Ma'am."

"Oh, I don't intend to feed them, dear Thomas," she answered, a hint of a smile. "I intend to play them."

Thomas didn't appear sufficiently convinced, but he would let it go for now. They would meet on this further, of that he was sure. Janice was not one to jump into something like this without collaborating with her staff and coming to some consensus.

"Yes, ma'am," he stated.

They stood in silence then, looking out across the clearing and into the surrounding forest.

The Outland was a strange world, filled with strange things and myriad possibilities.

Chapter Three

The trail was wide enough that Jake and Meara were able to walk side by side. They were traveling one of the main trails of the network of trails that connected several of the temples of the Outland. Two monks followed at some distance behind them, another two walked ahead. Ahead of these walked Master Peter.

It was near midday and they had been hiking since before dawn. The day was gray, the air cool; a thin mist drifted through the sparsely treed forest on either side of the trail. Jake felt each step in his ribs, bruised and still bound in bandages.

Upon further consideration, it might have been better had they waited another day or two and let

Peter and his group leave without them, and so giving Jake more time to heal.

The pain must have shown on his face and in his gait.

"Would you like me to ask them to stop for a bit, sir?" asked Meara. "We could all do with a rest."

"I'm good," said Jake. "We'll be stopping for lunch soon enough."

"Yes, sir."

They continued on in relative silence. They had spoken very little since leaving the temple, and their traveling companions were not much for casual conversation in any case.

The procession slowed then, without coming to a full stop, when the young monk that had gone ahead of the group reappeared. He stepped into line beside Peter as they continued walking. He spoke to Peter in a hushed voice.

Peter did stop then and looked back to the line of travelers spread out along the trail behind him. He waved Jake and Meara forward and waited.

"I'm afraid we will need to travel off the main trail for a time," he said calmly. "One of the bandit bands has established what Brother Oliver described as a semi-permanent encampment some short distance ahead of us."

Jake remembered having passed the trailhead of a side path about ten minutes back. He nodded over his shoulder and asked if that trail would take them around.

"Not directly, no. I suggest we go off trail here," said Peter. He indicated the forest to their left. He knew of a much narrower, less-defined animal trail that paralleled the main trail some half mile away, roughly following a small, meandering creek. They could follow that until they were well past the bandit camp.

Jake nodded silent agreement.

"Very good, then," said Peter. He indicated that Brother Oliver should lead the way. The young monk stepped off the trail and started into the forest.

Peter looked to Meara, then to Jake. He gave him a sympathetic smile.

"We'll break for lunch once we reach the creek," he said and then followed after Oliver.

"After you," Jake said to Meara.

It was late in the evening, nearing midnight. The Quigley Estate was quiet. A single, vintage ceiling fixture offered the only light in the kitchen.

Mrs. Hodges was puttering around the high-ceilinged kitchen, dressed in a thick, fluffy robe, well-worn slippers and a scarf to tie back her hair. She half-filled a tea pot and put it on the stove, turned on the burner. She set a box of tea bags on the center island counter and went to the cupboard to bring down a tea cup.

Mr. Griffin appeared in the doorway, dressed in an ankle-length housecoat.

"Mrs. Hodges," he said softly. "Are you having trouble sleeping?"

Mrs. Hodges turned quickly about, hand to her chest.

"Oh dear," she said, a heavy sigh. "You startled me."

"I do apologize." Mr. Griffin stepped over to the island counter and settled onto one of the tall stools.

Mrs. Hodges brought two tea cups down from the cupboard and set them onto the narrow counter next to the stove. She sat then opposite Mr. Griffin.

"I find a full night's sleep more difficult to come by these days, Mr. Griffin."

"Yes," said Mr. Griffin. "As do I."

"We be a couple of old fools, wandering about this old mansion at all hours, worrying about Master Quigley and young Jacob."

Mr. Griffin leaned forward and rested his arms on the counter.

"The boy has acquitted himself well enough," he said.

"And yet… here you are."

"Yes, Mrs. Hodges," sighed Griffin. "Here I am."

They sat silent for several moments. The teapot began its slow, growing whistle and Mrs. Hodges stepped over to the stove. She waited until the whistle reached a high pitch, then took the teapot off the heat. She placed a tea bag into each cup and poured.

"Chamomile," she said over her shoulder. "It should help with sleep."

"Thank you, ma'am."

Mr. Griffin watched Mrs. Hodges step back to the counter and set the cups down between them. Mrs. Hodges settled back onto her seat, absently dipped the tea bag in her cup.

"They've been gone a long while, Mr. Griffin," she said.

"They've been gone longer in the past, Mrs. Hodges; now and again."

"Six weeks is a long time with no word, all the same."

"I'll not start worrying just yet." Mr. Griffin carefully squeezed his tea bag, set it on the saucer and lifted the cup to his lips.

"And yet... here we are," said Mrs. Hodges.

"Yes." Mr. Griffin took a second sip of the tea, set the cup back onto the saucer. "Here we are."

Jake stood looking down at the small campfire, the flickering light of the flames reaching past him and out to the wall of trees and undergrowth that enclosed the clearing. Several of the monks that were traveling with him were sleeping nearby; several others stood watch, were little more than shadows within shadows in the surrounding forest.

It was late, well after midnight; the sky overhead was black and starless, the overcast from the day continuing deep into the night. Jake had just come off watch and wasn't yet ready to crawl under a blanket and return to sleep. Meara came into the clearing then, her own turn at watch also over. She stood beside Jake and looked down at the fire, held her hands out to try to catch what little heat rose from the flames.

"Hardly worth it," she mumbled softly, careful not to wake the sleeping monks.

"What's that?"

She gave a nod to the campfire, so small that it did little to provide warmth while putting out just enough light to attract the attention of anyone or anything within a hundred yards.

They were miles past the bandit encampment. Still, there were others out there, and other dangers.

"It's a psychological thing," said Jake. "You can't have a camp without a campfire."

"Yes sir," said Meara. She was sure that she had said that to him a long, long time ago.

She knelt down nearer the fire, seeking out what little heat emanated from the glowing coals beneath the flames. It felt good on her face.

Jake squatted onto his haunches, onto his heels, rested his elbows onto his knees, as he continued to stare into the fire.

"It will be good to be home, eh Meara?" he asked. "All the conveniences of home?"

"It will," noncommittally.

Jake looked up, looked over the fire and across to the world around them. They had spent weeks mapping this sector of the now much larger Outland, all with an eye as to how the village of Serpent's Keep might fit into this new world, what this new landscape might offer the village and what the village might have to offer this isolated new world.

"You've always appreciated the Outland more than I, sir," said Meara.

"And yet, here you are."

"Of course." She gave only the quickest glance over to Jake before looking again to the fire. "I couldn't very well let you stumble around out here on your own, sir. Who knows what might happen?"

Jake pushed down a grin, returned his focus to the glowing, shimmering coals.

"Thanks," he mumbled. He silently appreciated Meara's rare attempt at humor.

At least, he hoped it was humor...

"You're welcome," she answered.

As he had expected, Tobias had found the Lynhaur caves in the cliff wall deserted, the village of flying dragons set deep in the Great Ravine having been abandoned well ahead of the dissolution of the web. What he had hoped against hope, however, was that he might find a side passage, even a fraying thread, that might have survived and might still be connected to one of the Jahai villages. The Great Ravine had always been a focal point of the web and there had been the possibility, however small, that somehow some thread might have survived.

But Tobias had found nothing.

He reached down now, picked up several pieces of wood and tossed them into the fire, creating a cloud of sparks above the flames. He looked beyond the fire to the caves cliff wall. Khol had settled at the base of the wall for the night, dragons not being particularly fond of campfires.

Sitting around the campfire appeared to be a primarily human thing.

It would be morning soon. Even now, the cliff wall rising up behind Khol was beginning to lighten, shadows slowly being pushed aside, revealing the black mouths of the dozens of shallow caves that were set into the rough rock.

Khol shifted his weight, leaned forward and slowly rose up. He looked about the clearing, beginning to shade to gray but for the campfire, with Tobias sitting beside the fire.

He walked over and stood opposite the fire from the human.

"Have you slept at all, Tobias Quigley?" he asked.

"Enough, my friend," said Tobias. He looked up. The sky was just a shade lighter than just a few minutes earlier. "It will be morning soon."

"Yes," Khol stated flatly. He breathed noisily through his snout, looked carefully at Tobias. "What will you do now, Tobias Quigley?"

"I shall continue my search," said Tobias. "Beginning right after breakfast."

"I see. And where will your search take you?"

To some of my old stomping grounds, thought Tobias.

"I'm not sure just now," he said. "And what about you, friend Khol? What will you do?"

"I will seek out others as myself," said Khol. "There are certainly those who were left behind in the Outland at the close of the web."

"No doubt, no doubt." Tobias considered then. "Lamal has been seen."

Lamal, the Guardian at the ruined temple that had last been located along the Dark Path, had been a silhouette in the sky above the Outland in recent weeks, seen a number of times over the past several months. Quite to be expected, as the temple ruin was a part of the reintegrated Outland.

"I have seen Lamal with my own eyes," said Khol. "I was unfortunately not able to draw his attention."

"Unfortunate indeed," said Tobias. "I do have a suggestion, friend Khol."

Khol tilted his head slightly, a Jahai sign of curiosity. "Yes?"

"The temple ruin has likely remained Lamal's home base."

"Almost certainly."

"It is quite some distance from here," Tobias said, still considering. "What say you and I travel there together? I can continue my search along the way, and who knows what we might find once we get there?"

"I see," Khol said, thinking the idea through. "Perhaps others in my situation may have already sought out or will yet seek out Lamal's temple."

"Quite possible, indeed." Tobias turned his focus to the campfire before him. The flames flickered; there was a crackling sound as embers settled into the coals.

Khol took a step to one side, took several steps back. He shifted and slowly settled down, watched the human, studied the human. He tilted his head slightly.

Tobias caught the gesture while continuing to watch the fire. He reached out to the side, gathered up several sticks and tossed them into the fire.

"But first, breakfast," he said.

Chapter Four

TahLyn led the small group of Jahai across the gray, desolate landscape. She was of the Bentai species, a small figure alongside the two much larger reptilian-like Thrauhm Jahai that walked with her. Above them, a winged Lynhaur glided in slow circles.

The world around them was a featureless, near colorless plain spread out beneath a gray, featureless sky. They had travelled three hours from the landing and had found nothing, were now on their way back home.

Up ahead then appeared the dark silhouette of a short, squat feature.

One of the Thrauhm pushed out his overlarge head and gave a deep snort-like noise.

"I see it," said TahLyn. Glancing above, she watched the Lynhaur widen its circling, pushing nearer their target.

It took another minute's travel nearer for the silhouette up ahead to begin to take on its true shape. The obelisk stone was chest high to TahLyn, square with a smooth top. Their Lynhaur traveling companion had landed and had settled in beside the object, was placidly waiting for the others.

"Go home now?" it asked. It tilted its head.

"Yes," said TahLyn. "We go home now."

If the thread is still there, she thought, studying the obelisk. *We will find out soon enough...*

She looked calmly to her companions in a silent impetus. In response, each of the Thrauhm reached out to her and rested their clawed hands on her shoulders. The

Lynhaur ambled up beside them, placed a hand on them.

Ready...

TahLyn reached out and held a hand above the obelisk. She hesitated a moment, then lowered her hand onto the surface. The smooth stone felt cool against the thick skin of her palm.

There came the familiar rush of white empty. It washed over them, through them, past them...

A moment later...

They were standing beside a stone obelisk very similar to the one they had just left behind. This one stood a dozen yards off a wide trail that cut through a field of low, yellow brush.

They were back on the Dark Path.

This was the furthest they had managed to travel the Dark Path, and getting this far had been difficult, with each journey's success uncertain. The Path was disjointed, broken, in disarray. Travel would appear normal, untroubled, only to suddenly fragment, fall apart, and they would find themselves isolated, the world around them unrecognizable.

They had found a handful of side passages, each thread unreliable, leading to dead landscapes, uninhabited landscapes, with unfamiliar landings. To now, they had been unable to reach Aldwyn and his castle, this being one of their goals.

They started along the Dark Path towards home. After most of a day's travel they reached the tall, wooden double gate. One of the Thrauhm stepped forward and reached out, pounded on the gate.

They waited.

After several long moments they heard the wooden crossbar slide aside and the double gate opened. A young Bentai stood beyond the gate. He stepped to one side and gave a welcoming bow to the travelers.

"Thank you," said TahLyn, passing through. Her two Thrauhm companions followed closely behind her. The Lynhaur came last, passing overhead, flying above the gate, its wings spread wide, gliding in the general direction of the Jahai Village.

With the gate again locked, the Bentai on watch hurried forward to take the lead, escorting the returning team back into the village. They were met by Natan in the center of the plaza. The Jahai leader dismissed the escort to return to his duties. He then thanked the two Thrauhm companions and dismissed them as well.

"Attend me, TahLyn," he said then. He turned about and TahLyn stepped in beside him. They started back across the plaza. Natan listened as TahLyn detailed their latest journey into and along the Dark Path. The report was similar to those of the half-dozen previous reports she had presented.

As best as could be determined, the Dark Path and any threads were isolated, connected to nothing. The

Path and the village were alone, torn from the rest of the world, from the rest of the universe; they had been separated from the other Jahai as well, and from the Jahai home worlds.

And beyond this, the Dark Path and the Jahai village had been torn from the Outland.

Natan could only hope that his assistant Khol, his friend, was well.

That the Jahai Village and Dark Path had remained together had initially been considered most fortunate. The phenomenon that was the Dark Path had always been something special, something uniquely Jahai, uniquely of the Jahai Village.

It should now be their way home.

As yet, it was not. As yet, the Jahai Village and the Dark Path were alone.

"We will go out again, Natan," said TahLyn, having completed her report. "A day, and we will go out again."

They reached the doors of the Grand Hall. Natan stopped, turned about and looked out across the plaza. TahLyn, standing beside him, waited.

"Your opinion regarding the threads, TahLyn."

"Natan?"

"What few threads you have found have been broken and, if viable at all, they took you nowhere."

"That is so," said TahLyn. "Perhaps the next."

"Perhaps," sighed Natan.

TahLyn again waited. Natan grew distant, thoughtful.

"I would ask something of you, TahLyn," he said.

"Of course," said TahLyn. "I serve the Jahai."

"Thank you." Natan turned to look directly at her. "Gather what supplies you feel warranted for an extended journey; as much as you can carry."

"Yes, Natan."

"I wish for you take the Dark Path as far as it will take you."

"Yes, Natan." TahLyn hesitated. "Natan, we have traveled twice the distance previously known, without reaching its end."

"I know," said Natan flatly.

Natan asks for something more...

"I see," she said.

Natan turned his focus again to the plaza. Several Jahai were milling about; it was otherwise quiet.

"Take it to its end," he stated. *Find the castle, my young friend. Find Aldwyn...*

"Yes, Natan." TahLyn gave a brief, abbreviated bow of the head. "We will journey to its end."

Natan gave an acknowledging nod without turning to look at her.

"Thank you, TahLyn."

It was good to be home.

Master Peter finished his meeting with the temple staff, in which he was assured that there had been no major disasters in his absence, and stepped out of the conference room and into the hall. He followed the passageway into the west side wing, nodding acknowledgments to brother monks that he passed along the way. He took the narrower hall down to the medical room. He found Jacob Quigley sitting on the examination table, where he was being attended to by Brother Drake, the temple's elderly medical administrator.

Jacob lifted his arms to allow Drake to wrap his bruised ribcage with fresh bandaging.

"How does he look, Brother Drake?" asked Peter. "Will the young man survive?"

"The recent journey will delay his healing, Master Peter," said Drake, a bit grumpily.

"I'm fine," said Jake.

"He is well enough." Drake finished the wrap. He stepped aside and handed Jake his shirt.

"Good, good." Peter stood before Jake. "You are welcome to stay with us for as long as you have need, Jacob."

"I appreciate that, but I'm anxious to get home," said Jake.

"I understand, of course."

"Nonetheless," Drake interjected. "A few days rest would be best."

"Thank you, Brother Drake," said Jake. He began putting on his shirt. "Meara and I will be heading to the village in the morning."

Drake shook his head as he began gathering the old bandages and his medical gear. *To be expected...*

Peter gave a sympathetic nod. "Of course, of course."

"I'm half a day from Mrs. H's kitchen," Jake slid off the examination table. "*It be calling to me.* I have no choice but to answer."

"Then answer the call you must," said Peter. He took a step back to the door, stopped and looked back. "But I would rather you didn't go alone. The well-traveled path from here to Serpent's Keep might not be safe, what with all that has been happening these last few months. I will ask two or three brothers to tag along."

"That is not necessary, Brother Peter."

"Nonetheless."

Jake finished buttoning his shirt. "Sure. Much appreciated. Have you seen Meara?"

Peter continued to the door. "I believe she is in the dining hall."

There was no movement. Short, thick tufts of grass and weeds grew in the seldom-traveled trail. A wall of trees and brush pushed up against one side of the trail; a field of tall, yellow grass spread wide along the opposite side. The afternoon sun shimmered orange-yellow against the pale blue sky.

The faint hint of a breeze began then, evident only by the slight wave of the dry grass, as yet the only sign of movement.

A sound then, distant, indistinct, drifted across the silence.

More moments then... it was a man's voice; casual, conversational. No words could yet be discerned.

Two figures appeared far down the trail, walking side by side. As they drew slowly nearer, one could be seen as human, the other a Bentai Jahai.

Long seconds later, the two ever nearer... the human was Tobias Quigley, the Jahai was Khol. Tobias traveled now with a tall, wooden staff, made from a six foot long tree limb, slightly gnarled, slightly crooked, freshly cut and trimmed.

Tobias was doing most of the talking. He was accustomed to traveling alone and was perfectly happy on his own; he actually enjoyed the solitude. He found himself a bit uncomfortable when traveling with a companion, whether it be his nephew Jake or in this case with friend Khol. And for some reason he felt it his duty to fill the quiet that he otherwise preferred.

Khol, for his part, was content to walk in silence and didn't really understand Tobias' need to fill the void.

Khol didn't notice that Tobias had stopped talking. He did sense that the human had slowed his pace. Tobias slowly came to a stop, then; he held a staying arm out to Khol.

Khol reached out with all his senses. He saw nothing in the forest of trees to their left, saw no movement in the field to their right but for the slight wave of grass being generated by the breeze.

He listened. His keen hearing caught the occasional stirring and chirping of small animals, the brush of wind across the grass.

Khol caught a smell then in the breeze; a musty animal scent that shouldn't have been there.

He looked side-glance to Tobias. Tobias gave an acknowledging nod without looking to his companion. He was focused on shadows in the trees a dozen paces or more ahead on the left. Khol could sense that Tobias was readying himself to respond to an impending threat.

With hardly a sound then, two *smart wolves* leapt out of the trees and onto the trail some twenty feet ahead. Tobias stood ready, unmoving, watching.

These wolves were bigger, bulkier than the normal wolf, with broader shoulders. Their heads were large, their faces almost flat but for the snout.

And their eyes betrayed that something was going on in there.

The lead wolf, a hand taller than the other, took a cautious step forward, stood his ground and studied Tobias and Khol.

"Hello, young friend," Tobias stated calmly.

The lead wolf showed no response; he stood silent, watching, waiting.

Tobias heard the slightest of sounds behind them; paw pads dropping onto the trail as one or more wolves leapt out of the forest.

Khol half turned his head just enough to see that there were indeed two wolves watching from a dozen paces back along the trail.

"Two more," said Khol quietly, looking forward again.

"Thank you," said Tobias, continuing his focus on the lead wolf.

"Uh, huh…"

Tobias gave a thin smile.

"You are far from home, friend," said Tobias to the lead wolf. "And you are on your own."

The lead wolf tilted its head a few degrees, gave a slight twitch.

"That is it then, is it?" asked Tobias. "Striking out on your own?"

The lead wolf took another cautious step forward, straightening its head. The wolf behind it made no move.

There was no sound from the two smart wolves standing in wait behind Tobias and Khol.

"Tobias?" Khol prompted, hardly a whisper.

Tobias gave a nod to the lead wolf.

"Our young friend there," he said. "A young Alpha. And he is no longer comfortable taking orders from the Leader of the Pack."

"Yes?" asked Khol.

"He is looking at starting a pack of his own." Tobias turned half about, glancing back at the two smart wolves behind them. He looked forward again, gave the hint of a smile to the young lead wolf. "And I suspect there are more than just the four of you."

The lead wolf lifted his head, kept his focus on Tobias.

"Yes," said Tobias. His eyes drifted briefly to the shadows in the trees on their left. "I believe you will do well, my friend."

Khol shifted, leaned near Tobias.

"Does he know who you are, Tobias Quigley?" he asked. "Are we... all right?"

As they watched, the lead wolf took another cautious step forward. It tilted its head, straightened, gave another twitch.

"He knows who I am," said Tobias. "As for our health and welfare... that has yet to be determined."

Khol gave a low grumble, gave a studied gaze to one and the other of the wolves in front of them.

Tobias held his staff forward, planted it firmly on the hard surface of the trail.

"As I respect the Pack of your youth, my young friend, I respect the Pack that you now lead," he said.

The lead wolf gave a brief jerk of the head. It took another soft step forward, now near striking distance. The wolf behind him also took a step forward.

Tobias held his ground.

"I suggest that you and I come to the same accord as I at present hold with your brethren."

The wolf made no movement at first, gave no indication that he had even heard Tobias. Several moments more, and he took one step back, stopped.

He warily eyed the human and the Jahai.

"Tobias Quigley?" Khol asked.

"The young leader considers," said Tobias.

Another several long moments...

The lead wolf gave a slight snort. His head twitched. A moment more, he turned suddenly and leapt off the trail, back into the shadows of the bordering forest. His companion quickly followed, as did the two behind Tobias and Khol.

Tobias heard the faint rustling of perhaps a half a dozen more smart wolves moving deeper into the forest.

Khol let out a long grumbling sigh.

"I believe his agreement with you was made half-heartedly, Tobias Quigley," he said.

"I believe you are right," said Tobias. He brought his staff back and started forward. "I suggest we put some significant distance between us and this new Pack."

"A good idea," said Khol.

"And I believe we will have to go off trail soon," Tobias continued. "Assuming we are where I think we are."

"I'm good with that."

Tobias gave a grin.

"Yes. It wouldn't hurt."

Chapter Five

Master Peter enjoyed watching the sunrise from his temple's roof deck.

No. Not the sunrise. Rather, Peter liked to view the Outland through the sunrise. He came up onto the roof deck before dawn most mornings whenever he was home, whenever his early morning duties allowed.

The world was in predawn gray. Mist drifted slowly through the trees and about the temple grounds, rolling across the clearing that was spread out before the front steps of the sanctuary. A slight, damp breeze brushed Peter's face. It was cool but refreshing. His heavy monk's robes kept him warm.

He turned to look to the east. The village of Serpent's Keep lay in that direction, just half a day's easy hike. As he watched, rays of color formed on the horizon and then streaked across the forest canopy and to the temple. The clouds of mist that were rolling through the trees filled with orange and red.

He heard the door behind him open and gently close. Moments later Brother John stood beside him.

"Good morning, Master Peter," said John.

"Yes it is, John."

John looked admiringly out across the surrounding forest.

"It is good to be home," he said.

"It is." Peter glanced briefly at John, again then to the view. "Still, it was a successful journey, wouldn't you say?"

"I suppose it was."

"Come now, John," said Peter. "Our visits to our brethren's temples. It was quite an education."

"Yes sir," said John. "It was."

Peter let his gaze drift to the north. He nodded slowly then, half lost in thought.

"The North Temple," he said finally.

"Master?"

"It's waiting for us."

"It will happen, Master Peter."

"Of that I have no doubt, John," said Peter. "It will be a journey unto itself."

"Have you found anything further?" John knew that Master Peter had already spent time in the library since their return, likely researching the six temples, the temple in the far north isolated from the others.

"A bit," said Peter. He shrugged then. "In fact, not so much."

"You will, sir."

More likely we will just strike out and hope for the best, thought Peter.

Hearing the temple's front door down below them open and close, followed then by the sound of the shuffling of feet in the otherwise quiet morning, both Peter and John leaned forward and looked down into

the clearing in front of the sanctuary.
A group had started down the steps
from the porch. Stepping away then,
they started into the open, a robed
monk leading the way. Jake and Meara
were following closely behind, with
two more brothers bringing up the
rear.

"There they go," said Peter.

They were on their way to Serpent's
Keep. John looked up, looked east
across the treetops. They should be
there by midday.

Peter watched as the group
reached the far side of the clearing
and entered the trailhead,
disappearing into the trees.

"You can still catch up to them,
John," he said. "Join them."

John had family in Serpent's Keep.
They hadn't been all that keen on
John becoming a monk, and John had
only recently begun reaching out to
them after years apart. He had visited
with them twice in recent months.

"Not necessary, sir," said John.

"All right," said Peter. "The offer stands."

"Thank you."

"Though…" Peter stared at the empty trailhead, raised a brow. "You'll have to hurry."

The trail between the temple and the village of Serpent's Keep was well traveled, the most traveled path of all the Outland. Until recently it had also been considered relatively safe, at least safer than many of the other, more obscure trails of the Outland.

Now though, the reintegration of the far-flung components of the greater Outland had brought with it a whole new bunch of dangers.

It was so sad…

"Thank you no, sir," said John. "I believe I'll skip this trip."

Peter nodded in answer. He returned his gaze to the eastern horizon. The sunrise was complete, the golden orb now sitting atop the trees. The dawn colors were fading to pale blue and gray.

Peter turned away from the roof's edge.

"I'll be in the library," he said and started to the door.

Janice was kneeling in the shadows of the trees, huddled behind brush. She looked out across the narrow dirt road to the Farm. The morning mist that had been hovering above the fields had burned off, and the day looked as though it was going to be clear if a bit cool.

Martin was kneeling beside her, studying the scene in silence. Beside Martin was Kailee, Thomas' young assistant. She was there in Thomas' stead, he having insisted that he should remain at the Rhetani-occupied temple and continue with the security enhancements. Kailee was in her mid-twenties, though looked even younger. She had been part of Thomas' small group since well before the recent events surrounding the shutting down of the gateways and then the rejoining of the Outland.

Janice and her two companions had been considering the situation at the Farm for several hours. From what they had been able to observe, security was light, though greater than it had been in the past. A pair of well-armed security walked the perimeter of the village farm. Several others, nowhere to be seen at the moment, walked routes in and about the cluster of buildings in the heart of the farm.

There was very little movement, not so much as a breeze to stir the grass in the nearer fields. The only activity was near one of the larger farm buildings, where several farm workers were gathered beside a row of wagons. Two of them looked to be finishing up loading one of the wagons as two others stood nearby.

"I don't know, Janice," said Martin. "Taking it wouldn't be a problem. Security isn't that strong, and there aren't all that many hands. But keeping it, that's something different." He leaned forward and looked down the dirt road. "We'd likely have company before long."

Janice's expression remained unchanged.

Kailee gave a confirming nod.

"I'm afraid he's right, ma'am," she said. "We are so few, and the layout of the farm being what it is... we would never hold it."

Janice's expression continued to remain unchanged. Her focus was solely on the goings-on hundreds of yards distant, near the cluster of buildings.

"Ma'am?" Kailee prompted. "Why take the farm at all? Why not just take the wagon train while it's en-route to the village? No fuss."

"We're not looking for supplies, Kailee," said Janice coolly. "We're looking to establish the Rhetani presence."

"Yes, ma'am," said Kailee. "Of course."

Janice slid back a bit further into the shadows. So did Martin and Kailee. Janice looked to her companions, then again to the farm.

"We need to have a meet with the bandits," she said.

"A meet?" asked Martin.

"The bandits?" asked Kailee. "Ma'am?"

"The bandits," said Janice, giving a slow nod. "Perhaps hire them first to assist with the takeover, then keep 'em on as security."

Martin looked very skeptical.

"Oh, Janice…"

"Yes," she sighed. "I know."

Charles Victor, the manager of the village farm, stood with arms folded, watching the hands tie the canvas cover over the lead wagon. Charles was in his sixties, his hair beginning to gray, his skin weathered from half a century working in the fields, most of that time managing the farm.

His assistant, half Charles' age, stepped up beside him, beside the wagon. He pulled at the edge of the canvas as if to ensure that it was secure.

"Do you see them?" he asked Charles, pointedly ignoring the three people that were huddled in the shadows of the trees on the other side of the dirt road, several hundred yards distant.

"Yes," said Charles. He casually looked over at one of the hands, tying the line to keep the canvas in place. "I see them."

Jake was sitting in a wooden folding chair, a small wooden side table beside him on which sat a tall glass of iced tea. He was wearing a jacket, as the evening was rather cool.

He was home, the Quigley Estate. He was relaxing on the mansion's second floor deck, which was enclosed on three sides and looked out across the village and the village wall to the west. The temple was out there in the Outland. On very rare occasions one could see the gleam of the sun against the spire; not so today.

Several of the street lamps along the village's main thoroughfare were already lit against the dusk. Several windows were aglow, with warm light filtering through closed curtains.

The door behind Jake opened and quietly closed.

Mr. Griffin stood beside Jake then, looking out at the village.

"Are you sure you should be up and about, young sir?"

Jake picked up his glass of iced tea, took a drink, set it back on the table.

"I'm fine, Mr. Griffin," he said.

"Mrs. Hodges instructed you to rest." Mrs. Hodges had given him the medical once-over and redressed his wounds.

"I _am_ resting."

"Yes," Mr. Griffin said stiffly. "So I see."

Jake glanced up at the tall figure standing beside him, again looked outward.

"How's Meara?" he asked.

"Doing well, I understand. She is visiting her mother."

"That's good." Jake took another drink from his tea, leaned back in the chair, keeping the glass in hand.

"Anything from my uncle?"

"Nothing from Master Quigley," said Mr. Griffin. "That is not unexpected."

"No. I suppose not." Jake frowned. "Still..."

"Yes, sir," agreed Mr. Griffin.

Jake took another long drink from his iced tea.

A gentle slope fell away from the ridge down to a thinly wooded forest of oak and alder and evergreen. Broken building spires rose up from a shallow basin just beyond the trees; nestled in the basin was the temple ruin, a cluster of interconnected buildings, now little more than the jagged outlines of broken walls. It looked much as it had during Tobias' previous visit. But there were a few differences visible, even from this distance. He could see movement, several Jahai moving about in the ruin. He could see broken stone blocks now stacked, forming the structures of cave-like shelters.

Lamal was circling overhead, a winged silhouette set against an evening sky of fading blue with wide swathes of darker blue and violet and burgundy splaying out from the west.

"There is not much left," said Khol. He knew of this temple ruin, when it had been known to be reachable along the Dark Path, but he had never actually been there, had never seen it.

It felt somehow strange to Khol that he should visit it now that it was no longer a milestone on the Dark Path.

They took the switchback trail down the hillside, followed it then through the woods and straight on to the site of the ruin, finally then to a set of stone steps that led up to what had at one time been the front double doors of the temple. It was now nothing more than the splintered remains of a door jamb; they stepped through it to a foyer with no ceiling or walls, with the shards of tall, broken spires rising up on either side.

Spread out before Tobias and Khol were rotted wooden beams among broken stone and chunks of concrete, wall foundation footings outlining the vestiges of hallways and rooms and sleep cells. Set in amongst these were the simple structures that had recently been put together to serve as shelters.

A few yards to Tobias' left stood a large Thrauhm Jahai; reptilian, heavily muscled, its large head leaning cautiously forward. Its nostrils expanded and contracted, sniffing.

"Blood of Tobias," it stated brusquely. It tilted its great head, shifted its gaze to Tobias' companion. "Khol."

"It is good to see you, Mauch," said Khol.

"Welcome," Mauch said, then straightened. "You pass."

"Thank you, Mauch," said Khol, nodding. He and Tobias continued into the ruin.

A shadow passed over them and danced across the broken stone of the ruin. There came the thrumming sound of beating wings. Lamal hovered a moment ahead of them, drew his legs out and forward and grasped the top of a broken wall. He shifted around and settled atop the wall, facing the new arrivals.

He silently watched the human and the Bentai Jahai maneuver through the ruin and approach. He recognized the human.

"Tobias," he said.

"Hello, friend Lamal." Tobias indicated his companion. "This is Khol."

"Khol," said Lamal.

Khol gave an acknowledging nod. "Lamal."

Lamal looked again to Tobias.

"Something happened, Tobias Quigley," he stated matter-of-factly.

"Yes."

"We are no longer on Pelonar." Lamal lifted his gaze, looked outward, beyond the temple ruin that had been his home for so many years. "Outland."

"That is correct," said Tobias. "The Outland is again one. The temples have been brought together."

"Home," said Lamal.

"That it is, friend."

Lamal lowered his gaze, looked briefly to Tobias, then to Khol. He looked about the temple.

"Friends come. Some come. Some come."

"I am glad," said Tobias. He turned to Khol. Khol was looking about the ruin, noting his brethren moving about the remains of the sanctuary. He quickly identified three species of the Jahai, maybe ten or twelve individuals all total. Perhaps there were more beyond his view.

Khol sensed his friend Tobias watching him. He turned to him.

"This is good," he said.

"Yes, friend Khol," said Tobias. "It's a start."

Chapter Six

Janice stood at the top of the steps, hands clasped behind her back, waiting. The late afternoon was drifting into evening and the clearing before her was filling with shadow.

The doors of the Rhetani Temple opened behind her. Martin came out onto the porch and stepped up beside her. Janice ignored his presence.

They waited.

The air felt heavy, thick. After several cool days, this day had been warm, moist, with little to no breeze. It took a little more effort to breathe.

Janice heard movement in the trees beyond the clearing. From the sound, there were several people approaching, following the trail, avoiding the security trip wires.

Thomas appeared at the trailhead. He saw Janice and Martin standing atop the steps as he entered the clearing, his two fellow team members coming into the clearing behind him. He approached the stone steps and stopped. He placed one foot on the bottom step and looked up at Janice.

"Janice," he said.

"Hello, Thomas," she said then. "It is good to see you back safely. It went well?"

"They have agreed to meet with you," said Thomas.

He waved a hand for his team to step forward, indicated then that they should go inside. They climbed the steps, gave silent nods to Janice as they moved around her and Martin and went into the temple.

Janice kept her attention on Thomas. She indicated for him to continue.

"They are intrigued at the suggestion of an association," he said then. "They would like to hear more."

"They have agreed to the meeting arrangements?" she asked.

"Of course," said Thomas, climbing the steps. "They appeared to be amused by the neutral location proposal."

"Well, that's unsettling," said Martin.

Janice actually managed the hint of a smile, quickly let it fade.

"Thank you, Thomas," she stated. "You should go get cleaned up. Dinner is in an hour."

"Yes, ma'am." Thomas crossed the porch and went inside.

Janice looked side-glance to Martin. Another smile formed and then faded.

Something to say?

"Martin?" she prompted.

"I've said it before, Janice," said Martin. "You can't trust them."

Janice gave a tired sigh, frowned and looked out across the clearing. The shadows moving through the surrounding trees were growing darker, the sky overhead grayer.

"Thank you, Martin," she droned. "I shall keep that in mind."

Brother John opened the door to the library and quietly entered the room. The walls were lined floor to ceiling with shelves filled with old volumes. Midway down the room an entire section of the wall was covered with a honeycomb of diamond-shaped compartments filled with scroll tubes.

Master Peter was sitting at one of the several tables in the middle of the room. A lone pole lamp illuminated an unrolled scroll that was spread out across the table before him.

John moved quietly across the room and stood before the table facing Peter.

Peter leaned back in his chair.

"Good evening, John," he said, carefully rolling the scroll.

"Master Peter."

Peter slipped the scroll into its tube, stood as he fitted the cap.

"Is there a problem?" he asked.

"No sir."

Peter nodded absently as he walked over the scroll compartments. He slid the tube into its shelf and began looking through the shelves for another, very specific scroll.

"So?" he asked, somewhat distractedly.

"Well," John said hesitantly. "Not a problem so much as an increasing concern."

"Uh huh." Peter read the label on the side of tube. "Ah. This is it."

John followed Peter back to the table. "It is the Rhetani, sir."

"Uh huh." Peter sat at the table. He pulled the cap off the tube, reached in with two fingers and carefully pulled out the scroll. "I'm listening," he said, unrolling and spreading out the scroll. It appeared to be a skillfully detailed map.

"We have been observing an increasing amount of activity in and around the temple that they have occupied," said John. "Quite a lot of comings and goings."

"I see." Peter did look up from the scroll. "Any ideas on what they're up to?"

"It can't be good."

"Really? Why not?"

This caught John off guard. "Well... *um*... they are Rhetani, after all."

"Right." Peter returned to studying the scroll. "I'm surprised at you, Brother John."

"Yes, Master Peter." John appeared genuinely chagrined. "I'm a bit surprised myself. I apologize."

"Yes," Peter said, sighing. "Still; history would suggest that it would be best that we know what they are up to."

"Yes, sir."

"Surveillance continues, of course?"

"Of course," John stated firmly. "Discretely."

"Good, good," said Peter, the matter seemingly settled for now. Studying the scroll, he ran a finger across the parchment near the top left corner. "As best I have been able to determine, the North Temple is here…" He let his finger drift in a wide arc. "Somewhere."

Brother John hovered over the table and studied the diagram where Master Peter was indicating.

"Yes, sir."

"Mmm." Peter then slid his finger south several inches. "Our network of trails only gets us to here."

"That leaves a lot of uncharted country, Master Peter."

"That it does, my friend," said Peter. His brow furrowed as he continued to study the diagram. He glanced up then to John, gave him a slight grin. "Are you up for it?"

"Absolutely, sir."

"Good, good." Peter returned his focus to the map. He ran his finger in a circle over the top-left quadrant.

"Please ask one of our brothers to prepare a map of this area; something that we can take with us."

The midday sun shone through the one window of the café, the outside light shimmering dully across a wide swathe of the reddish-brown wooden floor, its surface incredibly smooth from decades of cleaning, sweeping, scrubbing, polishing, and tens of thousands of footsteps.

Nine small square tables lined three of the walls, with one of those tables set directly beneath the window. Six larger tables were evenly spaced about the floor. Salt & pepper shaker sets and wooden napkin holders were set at each table.

Cosmo Dante, the owner of the only bank in the village, was sitting at his regular table set against the back wall. A thin, middle-aged man was sitting at the table beneath the window. Both men were focused on their lunches.

Jake was at one of the tables in the center of room. At the moment he was working on a bowl of soup; a half sandwich was on a small plate beside the soup bowl.

Sparta came from behind the counter and walked over to Jake's table, refilled his glass of iced tea.

"How is everything, Jake?" she asked.

"Excellent, Sparta," said Jake. "My compliments to Wallace."

"I'll be sure to pass that along," she said and took the half-dozen steps over to Mr. Dante's table.

Sheriff Smith came into the café. Standing just inside the door, he looked briefly about the room before walking over and sitting at the table next to Jake's.

"Young Mister Quigley," he said. "How's the soup today?"

"Quite good, Sheriff." Jake set his spoon into the empty bowl and pushed the bowl aside. He picked up his sandwich, took a bite. "The ham and cheese isn't bad either."

"I'll hold you to that, sir," Sheriff Smith said lightly. He looked in Sparta's direction. Her attention was on Mr. Dante, but she did manage a quick glance to the sheriff. They exchanged nods and Smith looked again to Jake.

"I heard that you picked up a few scrapes and bruises your last trip out," he stated. "I trust you are well on the path to recovery."

"I'm fine, Sheriff. The extent of my injuries was exaggerated just a bit."

"That's good to hear; and it's good to see you out and about."

Both looked up then as Sparta approached.

"Sheriff Smith," she prompted. "How goes the day?"

"Most satisfactorily, Miss Vesper." The sheriff shifted in his chair and smiled. "I have it on good authority that today's soup and sandwich special is quite good."

"Far be it from me to argue with that, Sheriff," said Sparta. "An iced tea with that?"

"Why not?"

"Great." Sparta left to give the order to Wallace. He was visible through the food-up window, moving about in the kitchen.

Sheriff Smith shifted about again to look across to Jake.

"Say… Jake," he started. "I don't suppose you've run into Mason since you've been back?"

"I can't say I've had the pleasure." Jake took a swallow of his iced tea. "This is my first chance to get out of the house. Why do you ask?"

The sheriff considered a moment, then pointed to an empty chair at Jake's table. Jake waved him over and Sheriff Smith changed tables. He scooted his chair forward.

"Mason says that we need to find out what is beyond the Outland."

"Wasn't it Mason who first suggested that we were alone? That there is nothing out there?"

"Actually," the sheriff sighed. "What he told me, in no uncertain terms, which is suggestive on its own, is that we need to find out what has replaced the outside."

"Replaced?"

"Exactly."

"I see." Jake took a moment to consider. He stared at his tea glass, then again looked up at Sheriff Smith. "Are we talking about the Road here?"

"He insists that we send a team out."

"I thought you already did that."

"I did. And they went far enough out confirm that the Outland is alone."

"Then I'm not sure—"

"Mason insists there is something out there. And he insists that we must find out what it is."

"I see," Jake repeated. "I guess."

Jake had traveled that road a number of times when growing up, spending summers at the Quigley Estate from the time he was twelve through his mid-teens. His journeys by bus from the outside world to the front gates of Serpent's Keep had seemed normal enough to a young boy; or at least as normal as his uncle's unique and distinctive village.

"And you're thinking that I'm the one to check it out?" he asked.

"I don't want to push you into doing anything that you don't want to do, Jake."

"Really, sheriff; I don't know that that's possible."

A slight smile from the sheriff. "I suppose you're right about that. You are your uncle's nephew, Mister Quigley."

"I'll take that as a compliment."

"As it was intended." Sheriff Smith saw Sparta come around the counter with his lunch. He leaned back in his chair to make way for her.

"Here you are, Sheriff," said Sparta. She lifted the bowl of soup from the tray and set it on the table. She set the sandwich plate and iced tea beside the bowl.

"Thank you much, Sparta." He waited while Sparta set out his silverware.

"Enjoy." Sparta gave a smile and returned to behind the counter.

"I wish I could go myself Jake, but circumstances being what they are..."

"Not a problem," said Jake. "Really. I'm glad to do it."

The sheriff scooted forward and picked up his spoon.

"I do so enjoy the food here," he said. "I can't imagine it's as good as Mrs. Hodges' cooking."

"I come here for the change in scenery," said Jake.

"I hadn't thought of that. And that would no doubt be in between your jaunts into the scenic Outland." Sheriff Smith took a spoon of soup, groaned appreciatively.

"Well that would be a different matter entirely."

"Of course." Sheriff Smith set down his spoon, picked up his glass of iced tea. "To the Road, then?"

Jake raised his glass. "And to wherever it may lead."

TahLyn, the young Bentai Jahai, waited with the other three of her team at the edge of the Jahai Village plaza as Natan crossed the square and approached them. It was early morning, quite early for dragons, and so there were very few others about.

The winged Lynhaur standing beside TahLyn shifted anxiously, eager to be off. The two large Thrauhm, carrying the team's packs of supplies, waited patiently a few yards away, near the head of the path that would take them to the gate and on to the Dark Path beyond.

Natan reached the team.

"TahLyn. You are ready." It was a statement, not a question.

"We are, Natan."

"Very good." Natan looked briefly at the others of the team. "You are well supplied?"

"We have all we need and more," said TahLyn. She couldn't be sure of that, of course. This time out, they did not know how long they would be traveling the Dark Path.

As long as was necessary.

Natan spoke then to the entire team.

"The good will of all goes with you," he said. "To the journey's end."

"The Dark Path must have an end and we will find it, Natan," said TahLyn. "We will reach it; we will stand before Aldwyn."

Natan took a step back, and then another, and gave the team a slight bow of the head.

"Off then," he said.

TahLyn turned about without another word. Ahead of her, the

Thrauhm started into the trail. TahLyn and the Lynhaur followed. It took several minutes to reach the tall, wooden gate; before the gate waited another young Bentai. Seeing the team approach, he lifted the crossbar and set it aside, opened the gate. The two Thrauhm stepped to one side and let TahLyn and the Lynhaur pass through the gate first.

Standing beyond the gate, TahLyn noted a change in the Dark Path since their last visit. The world before them was grayer, murkier than before. The air felt heavier, the sky lay more heavily upon them.

The Dark Path most certainly didn't have a mind of its own, but it was almost as if it knew they were coming, knew what was to be attempted and wasn't at all happy about it.

"Not right," said the Lynhaur. It opened and closed its wings; a clear indication of its disquiet.

"A gloomy start, to be sure," said TahLyn. "But the path lay ahead; it is there for us to follow."

The gate closed behind them. TahLyn noted the sound of the crossbar being put back into place. She tilted her head then and gave an unspoken signal to the Lynhaur. The winged Jahai stepped forward, took another step and slowly spread its wings; several more steps then as it lifted from the trail and ascended into the sky.

For the eighth time in recent months, TahLyn started away from gate and onto the Dark Path.

This time there was but one purpose.

They would travel the Dark Path to its end. They would find and stand before the Ancient Guardian.

Chapter Seven

Master Peter had never traveled this part of the Outland. But then, up until a few months ago this part of the Outland had existed in some other landscape, on some other plane.

There was a trail here, having been created by monks who had worked nonstop these past months to connect the temples that had been brought back together with a network of well-defined trails. Peter walked the wide trail now, with Brother John walking beside him. They were quiet for the most part; what few conversations they had spoken had been in low voice. Two young monks walked ahead of them, one behind the other. The two others of their small group followed a few yards behind Peter and John.

The world was eerily quiet, even for the Outland. The trees here were the same trees as the rest of the Outland, the brush the same as the brush in the forest undergrowth around Peter's home temple.

And yet, this Outland felt different. It even sounded different.

It wasn't different. Peter knew that it wasn't. And yet...

The two monks walking ahead of him stopped. One spoke briefly to the other, then both looked back to Peter and waited for him to reach them.

"This is it, Master Peter," said one of the monks. He looked off trail, to the north.

So this was where they would have to leave the trail, to walk the forest floor, and hope to find the North Temple, still miles distant. They could easily miss it. They could easily pass by it to the left or to the right and never see it.

Peter looked to where the brother monk had indicated, into the forest. According to the map that had been copied from the scroll that Peter had found, this was their route to the long lost temple. It looked no different than any other part of the Outland; same trees, same undergrowth, same shadows; same mote-filled rays of sun streaking through the canopy down to the forest floor.

It gave him the heebie-jeebies.

"Lead the way, brother," he said.

The monk gave Peter a nod and stepped off the trail, the second monk following. Peter held a hand out for John to go next, and Peter followed after, with the others of the group bringing up the rear.

They were quickly enveloped in the shadows and the shifting sunrays beneath the forest canopy. The sound of their footfalls on the mulchy forest floor was surprisingly loud in the otherwise silent world, wafting out and away through the surrounding trees and brush.

They traveled single file in a generally northerly direction for several hours, occasionally having to veer left or right to work their way around natural obstacles. No one spoke. Now and again they heard the sounds of small animals moving about in the brush or the mulch, the wisp of a breeze drifting through the forest.

In the late afternoon Peter noticed a large dark shadow far up ahead, the silhouette coming into and out of view through the trees. As they drew nearer, he saw that it was a hillock of a sort, a cluster of granite stones rising up from the forest floor. Standing before it, the mound was eighty feet wide, thirty feet high. The crown was still well below the top of the canopy. It had the look of a massive pile of large granite rocks dumped in the forest and then left behind.

Peter looked at the others of the team. They were already beginning to walk along the base of the mound, starting to work their way around it.

"Hold up," he said. He considered for a few moments, looking carefully at the mound of granite. He began scrambling up the rock face then, finding handholds and footholds.

"Master Peter?" John asked, questioning.

"A moment, John."

Peter worked his way to the top of the hillock. The summit, such as it was, was fairly wide, with numerous pockets and bulges. The hilltop was wide enough to accommodate the six of them with plenty of room to spare. One of the pockets would serve well as a fire pit, with the surrounding stones offering seating. There was a broad, flat area that would work for sleeping.

Most importantly, it offered a view of the surrounding area and was defensible.

Just in case...

Peter looked up into the sky. It was beginning to gray. He moved to a high spot, stepped up and looked outward again. He wasn't able to see much above the canopy without stretching on tiptoes.

He stepped down and worked his way back to the edge of the hillock.

"Come on up," he said. "We'll spend the night here."

Khol walked slowly, carefully along the top of the broken wall. To his right was the temple ruin, bustling now with activity as debris was being cleared away and crude, almost cave-like dwellings continued to be put together. The Thrauhm Jahai were doing most of the heavy lifting, while the smaller Bentai such as Khol did most of the supervising and the directing.

He stopped midway along the wall; he watched the activity for a few moments more before turning about and settling down to look outward, away from the ruin.

It was midafternoon. The sky was dark gray, the air wet. It had rained off and on through much of the day, and looked to Khol that it would rain again before dusk.

A rough trail wound away from the wall below him and through the surrounding short brush ahead before disappearing into the stand of trees some hundred yards distant. The bare soil of the trail shimmered with the damp; the brush to either side of the trail was slumped heavy with moisture.

A figure appeared then, coming out of the trees. It was a human.

It was Tobias Quigley. He carried a light backpack on his back; a utility belt with canteen and knife sheath was strapped to his waist. He followed the trail toward the broken, jagged wall of the ruin, gave a wave to Khol as he approached.

Khol gave a half nod of his large head in response. He watched then as Tobias climbed the set of rough stairs that had been formed using a stack of broken, concrete chunks of wall, then took the several steps to the Bentai.

"Friend Khol," said Tobias. He was looking into the ruin, noting the activity. There was a large group of Thrauhm and Bentai at work deep within the ruin. A smaller group worked nearer, below and just to Tobias' left, where two Thrauhm were clumsily attempting to remove chunks of debris. It wasn't easy. Thrauhm were large and strong, but they weren't built for carrying heavy blocks.

"Was your day successful, friend Tobias Quigley?" asked Khol.

"Oh, I don't reckon I would call it that," Tobias said with a sigh.

"That is too bad. I am sorry."

Both stood silent then, looking into the ruin. The activity was a welcome distraction.

"Not that I expected to find anything," said Tobias at last.

"And yet you go out each day."

Tobias gave the suggestion of a smile. "That I do," he said.

"I suppose it is a human thing," said Khol.

"No doubt," Tobias said, chuckling lightly. "Hope, when all reason says no."

"I understand."

"I appreciate that, friend Khol."

This temple ruin, as all the temples, had been sent to an alternative plane when the Outland had been pulled apart. The difference here was that the temple ruin had also been a part of the Dark Path, a unique and rather ambiguous entity. With the return of this temple ruin as part of the Outland, might some connection to the Dark Path have come with it? If so, might Tobias be able to travel the Dark Path? If so, the Jahai Village waited for Tobias at one end, Aldwyn and his castle at the other.

It was increasingly obvious that Tobias was unlikely to see either. He had found no sign that any connection to the Dark Path had followed the temple ruin.

"What will you do now, friend Tobias Quigley?" asked Khol.

"Oh, I'll hang around a few days," said Tobias, considering. He indicated the work going on below them. "Maybe I can help."

"I am sure your help would be appreciated," said Khol. "And what will you do then?"

"I expect I'll be moving on. I should probably check in at home. I have been told now and then that folks worry about me."

When it came to human humor, Khol was never quite sure; friend Tobias Quigley's humor in particular. As such, he found it best to take whatever the human said at face value.

"Then check in you should, friend Tobias Quigley."

They fell into a comfortable silence then. The air smelled of the approaching late afternoon rain.

Khol didn't like rain.

Jake stood with his back to the wrought-iron front gate of the Quigley Estate, his small backpack at his feet. It was early morning and the sun had yet to show itself. The air was clear and clean from the rain of the day before.

The estate took up most of the north side of the narrow lane, the grounds enclosed by a high fence. Across the road was the village plaza, a park surrounded by its own tall wall. Jake could see the sprawling lawns and winding walkways of the park through the opening of the park's wide north entrance that was set into the wall directly opposite the estate.

Jake turned at the sound of the Quigley Mansion's door opening and closing. Looking through the estate's gate, he saw Meara standing on the porch. She was slipping into her backpack. The pack belt clipped into place, she took the steps down to the front walk. Jake opened the gate and she stepped through.

"Sorry I'm late," she said.

"You're not late. I'm early." Jake made sure the gate was locked, then picked up his own backpack and slipped into the straps. "Are you ready?"

"I sure am," said Meara. She looked back through the gate to the mansion. "Mrs. Hodges was not happy at missing you. She wanted to prepare a breakfast for you."

"Mrs. H always wants to prepare a breakfast for me," said Jake. "I do love that woman."

"Yes sir."

They started away from gate and walked down the center of the narrow lane toward the center of Serpent's Keep. Reaching the main thoroughfare, they turned left and walked to the village's main gate. They met no one along the way. The village was for the most part still asleep.

Civilian guards stood to either side of the open double gate. They gave Jake and Meara simple nods of acknowledgement as they passed through. Mason stood alone half a dozen steps ahead. He looked ready to go. He was dressed in old jeans and long-sleeved shirt, carried a faded and frayed backpack. His hiking boots, however, were quality and looked to be broken in, ready for the journey that lay ahead.

"Good morning, Mason," said Jake, stepping up beside him. He looked up the Road ahead of them.

"Hello." Mason did not look to Jake. His focus remained outward, beyond the village, almost as if he was able to see what waited out there for them.

Meara kept her distance from the two men, some two paces behind them. Mason had always been vocally over-protective of Meara, of *Mr. Gyles' little girl,* and that had always rubbed her the wrong way.

She chose instead to keep her distance. She watched and listened as Jake tried to strike up a conversation with Mason. She thought that odd, really. Jake was well-liked by most who met him, and he was friendly enough, but he wasn't all that talkative.

She heard Jake ask one question and then another. Mason gave one word responses each time. Jake eventually gave up, gave a final nod and joined Mason in simply looking silently out at the world beyond the village.

It was another couple of minutes before the sheriff came through the gates, escorting the last two of the team that were going on this journey. Meara knew them both, of course; the village was a small community after all. Betty was a full-time member of the civilian guard, young and smart. She knew her business. Carlo was a bit older, somewhere in his late forties. He owned the handmade furniture shop, and sometimes worked guard duty for the wagon convoys coming from the Farm.

Sheriff Smith stood beside Meara as the others continued past, giving Meara good-morning nods on their way to Jake and Mason.

"Good morning, Meara," he said.

"Sheriff," she acknowledged.

"I wish I was going with you." He looked passed the others to the Road, then up into the sky. "The rain stopped. It should be a nice day."

"Uh, huh." Meara looked from the others to the sheriff. "What do we expect to find out there?"

"I haven't a clue."

"Then what are we doing?"

"This is Mason's little get-together."

"Sheriff... that's crazy."

Sheriff Smith grew thoughtful.

"Mason thinks there's something out there," he said then, giving a nod in Mason's direction. "He's probably right. He often is."

Meara had known Mason her entire life. As eccentric as he was, as peculiar as he was, she had to admit that his... *observations*... were weirdly accurate.

Still...

"And?" she asked.

"And..." The sheriff reconsidered. "Listen, whatever Mason's motivation, I would like to know what's out there, whatever it is. It might help us, it might not. Whatever, I think it best that we know. Don't you?"

Meara stared ahead, watched as Betty and Carlo continued to get acquainted with Jake.

"Hmm," she said noncommittally. She saw then Jake turn and look in her direction. He was ready to go. "That's it, then," she said to the sheriff. She shifted her backpack, adjusted the belt.

"Good luck to you, Miss Gyles."

"Thanks," she said. "See ya."

Meara joined the others. Sheriff Smith watched them from a distance as they prepared to depart. Jake looked back at him, gave him a wave. The sheriff gave a pensive wave in response.

Jake led the way, starting down the Road; the same road that he had traveled each summer by bus when he came to Serpent's Keep to visit his mysterious Uncle Tobias.

A young man came through the gate and walked up to the sheriff. Geoff occasionally helped the sheriff, though he most often worked as an apprentice to Numidia, the village blacksmith.

"They're off, then?" he asked, watching the team continue away, down the Road.

"That they are." Sheriff Smith turned and started back toward the gate. "What is it, Geoff?"

"The Farm is under observation, Sheriff." Geoff followed quickly beside the sheriff. "They're being watched.

Mister Victor has seen 'em. They're spying on 'em from across the road."

"I see." Sheriff Smith stopped, quietly considered. "That can't be good."

"No, Sheriff. That's what I thought."

"All right." The sheriff started again, passing through the gate and into the village. "Let's put together a team. Get 'em to the Farm."

"Yes sir."

"And find Wanda," said the sheriff. "Ask her to drop by my office at her earliest convenience."

"Yes sir."

Wanda was the head of the Civilian Watch. She was in her late sixties, gray hair turning silver; she ran the Watch with an iron fist well-fitted inside a foam glove.

Well into the village now, Sheriff Smith stopped again. He put his hands into the pockets of his light jacket. He looked up into the heart of Serpent's Keep. The sun was coming up, the early rays of dawn shimmering along the bricks and flagstones of the main thoroughfare. There were a few people out and about now, the day just getting started.

It won't stop with the Farm, he thought to himself. *They'll bring it here...*

"On your way, Geoff," he said.

The narrow dirt road wound its way through a landscape of grassy fields, with only an occasional twisted, ancient oak tree or thicket of yellow and brown brush to disturb the scene. The air was still, the morning sun already warm. Now and then Jake heard the buzz of insects, but mostly there was only the sound of their own footfalls, the sound of his own breathing.

Jake had never traveled this road on foot. He had only seen this passing landscape through the scratchy windows of the bus, through his eyes as the young boy visiting his uncle over the handful of summers that now seemed so long ago.

The old bus had come from another time, an old, creaky vehicle out of the 1940s. It was easy now to be drawn back to those trips from the real world to the village; the smell of aging plastic and worn leather, of hot motor oil. The windows, warm to the touch; the sound of sheet metal popping in the summer heat; the dull drone sound of the engine; the grumble of the tires on the dirt road.

Jake had almost always been alone on the bus but for the elderly driver; it has always been the same driver: an old man in faded blue slacks and shirt, his silver hair pushing out from under a faded blue cap; pallid skin, dull gray eyes. He always had a smile and a nod for Jake when the boy climbed on board, was always quiet en route, never speaking to his lone passenger.

And then one summer, Jake didn't travel to Serpent's Keep. Reaching his middle teens, Jake's life in the real world grew too busy to spend his summer months at the Quigley Estate.

Several years later, Jake grown then to a young man, came the letter: Tobias Quigley had passed away, or so it was thought, and he had left his entire estate, and his quest, to his nephew Jacob Quigley.

And so Jake's final journey down the Road, an ethereal journey from the real world to the almost otherworldly village of Serpent's Keep; a last journey taken in the antique bus, driven by an ancient driver with gray eyes and a faded blue cap.

The bus had left him at the front gate of the village before disappearing back down that dusty road. Jake had stepped through the gate and into another world, a world that he had somehow never truly seen during those summers' past, that he could never have imagined; that could never have existed in the real world.

He had entered his uncle's world. Now Jake's world...
So much had happened between then and now.

Jake listened to his soft footfalls on the dusty road, to the gentle breeze brushing across the tall, yellow grass of the sprawling fields to either side, took in the warm smell wafting up from the grass and out across the road.

Jake slowed, stopped. He took a moment to let all his senses reach out to all the elements of the morning. It was all so different when on foot; not at all as it had been to that young boy looking through the dull, faded glass of the windows of the old bus.

"Is something wrong?" asked Meara.

It took a moment for Jake to come back from wherever his distant thoughts had taken him, to realize that someone had spoken to him, had asked him a question.

He looked at Meara, standing beside him, then to Mason and the others of the team, standing several steps behind him.

"No." He turned from them, looked again up the dirt road; there was another slow curve up ahead, and then a long straight stretch. "Sorry."

He started forward again. Meara fell in beside him.

Mason looked to Betty and Carlo, gave a grumpy frown and followed.

Chapter Eight

Master Peter was only half listening. Brother John was talking in a hushed tone, as the heavy quiet of the surrounding forest demanded. The younger monk was speculating, not for the first time, on what they might expect when they finally found the lost North Temple.

Peter thought it unusual, really. Voicing such speculation was not in Brother John's nature. The near-ethereal atmosphere of this northern Outland that they now traveled must have been playing with his unspoken thoughts.

Peter stopped. He listened now, fully, to something that had brushed at his senses, to something coming from somewhere far past Brother John.

John turned and looked back to Peter.

"Master Peter?"

Peter let his hearing reach out across the forest floor. The others of the team stopped, did their best to hold their silence. John tried to hear what Master Peter had heard.

He heard nothing.

He looked curiously at Peter, shook his head.

Peter was sure that he had heard something that was not of the forest; not the breeze drifting across the floor, not the small animals that scurried about.

Something. There had been something out there...

Again, the breeze across the floor, through the brush, through the leaves of the canopy. A little animal was scurrying nearby through the mulch of the forest floor.

And that was it. Whatever it was, whatever he had heard… it wasn't there anymore.

"Never mind," Peter said at last.

He started forward again. John stepped up beside him, the others followed behind.

Three young men were huddled in the shadows, kneeling behind thick brush. They wore dark green robes, their hoods pulled up over their heads; monk robes, though different in style and color than those of the group of monks they were secretly observing.

The sounds of soft voices carried across the forest floor from the strangers being watched. The two walking at the head of the group were in quiet conversation; the others following their leader and his assistant walked in silence.

These monks traveling from another land had been seen

descending Granite Mound after
spending the night there, and had
been under observation ever since.

They were in all likelihood brethren
from one of the temples that had
been separated from their own so
long ago. By all indications they were
traveling to the Temple. They didn't
look to be a threat, were likely seeking
out lost brothers following the recent
upheaval.

They would nonetheless continue
to be closely watched.

The three observers slid slowly
back, moving deeper into the
shadows. They slipped away then,
traveled quickly and silently, and
hurried to move out ahead of the
strangers.

Janice slowly circled the clearing,
walking around the tall stone that
stood in its center. She was looking
outward, studying the perimeter,
looking for possible threats. Could

someone hide there? Could someone attack from over there?

She slowed as she pointed to a thicket, waved her hand. A young woman stepped up to the brush and began clearing it away. A young man was already clearing brush away from another location.

Janice turned finally to the stone itself. Martin and Thomas stood to either side of her. Thomas studied the stone as Martin watched Janice.

The clearing was half a day's march from their Rhetani temple. The stone looked very similar to those of the gateways that had been tied directly to Serpent's Gate, those that had gone silent when Jacob Quigley had brought together the Serpent's Gate artifacts.

This stone, however, stood in a clearing in a segment of the Outland that had until recently existed in a whole other world, in another plane. Janice had heard nothing of such portals existing in the other segments of the Outland. Had this been an actual gateway? Had the act of bringing the Serpent's Gate artifacts together reached out as far as the lost lands?

Janice stepped forward and rested a hand against the rough rock. It was cool to the touch. She brushed her hand across it, brought her hand back and looked at her fingertips, rubbed them together. She turned about and looked again about the clearing. The targeted vegetation had been cleared away. All looked ready.

Thomas glanced up into the sky, then to the trailhead opening in the perimeter. The opening was shrouded in shadow.

"Any minute now, ma'am," he said.

Janice acknowledged the observation with a nod.

Someone appeared in the trailhead then. The woman was another of Janice's team. She stepped into the clearing and moved to one side, stood out of the way.

They're coming...
Janice heard them then, following the trail, coming nearer. A few more moments and shadows appeared. A figure then; a large man entered the clearing, looked quickly about. Satisfied, he moved aside. Another figure, then another, stepped into the clearing.

Five then, finally; four men and a woman. Their clothes were ragged, could definitely use a wash, as could the bandits themselves.

One man stepped forward, ahead of the others.

Thomas leaned nearer to Janice. "Ma'am," he mumbled under his breath.

That was the leader, then.

Janice gave only a slight welcoming nod to the man.

Thomas cleared his throat. "Welcome, Captain," he stated formally.

Captain looked to be in late forties. He had rugged features, bristling whiskers, and sharp eyes that looked always to be amused by what they were seeing.

"Thomas," Captain stated coolly, those sharp eyes remaining on Janice.

"I present Janice," Thomas offered. "Principal of the Rhetani."

"So I hear," said Captain. He looked about the clearing, then at the stone behind Janice. "Interestin' choice for a meeting."

"We like it," said Janice, her tone firm, strong.

Only then did Captain again move forward. He stopped two paces from Janice, his focus now on the stone.

"I 'been here coupla' times," he said. "Weird rock."

"Yes," said Janice, not deigning to look behind her. She had already seen the stone, time now to focus on the subject at hand.

Captain spread his feet, taking a solid stance. He folded his arms across his chest.

"So. Whatcha got? What's the deal?" he asked. Behind him, his team formed a line against the perimeter of the clearing, spacing well apart.

"I propose a temporary alliance, you and I," said Janice.

"Yeah…"

"You are of course familiar with the Village Farm?"

Captain took a moment to consider where this might lead. His eyes sparkled. There was a twitch at the corner of his mouth. There was almost but not quite a smile.

"And you are suggesting…" the sentence drifted.

"I am." Janice moved her gaze across the faces of those standing in line behind Captain. She focused again on Captain. "It could be of benefit to us both."

"No doubt." Captain lifted a hand from this folded arms, raised a finger. "Point of order, oh Principal of the Rhetani. Why do we need you?"

"I would argue that the greatest benefit to you would be to actually take possession of the Farm, not just grab a bag of potatoes and run. Such would be better accomplished by us working together, you and I; such details would need to be worked out, of course."

"Of course." Captain frowned. "Sounds like a lotta work to me."

Janice had expected as much.

"Right," she sighed. "And then of course there is the Village."

This got Captain's attention. For a moment this showed on his face, but was as quickly masked. "Yeah?" he urged.

"A percentage of the spoils," she said, smoothly.

"Again." Captain raised a brow. "Why do we need you?"

"You and I both know that taking Serpent's Keep would be a far from simple matter."

"Then why bother? Why not just hit
the Farm, take what we want and
quietly depart?"

"I want the Village," Janice stated
calmly. "You quite obviously need
what the Farm has to offer. We both
do."

"Uh, huh." Captain mulled that over.
"And ya' got a plan."

"I do."

"Uh, huh." Another few moments to
consider. "That percentage of which
you dangle. It's gonna have ta' be
pretty big."

Behind him, the big man grinned
broadly. The others maintained their
stone expressions.

Janice let a gentle smile show.

"I feel certain that we can work out
an arrangement that will be
satisfactory to us both," she said.

Camp had been set up alongside
the Road; the road and the camp
shimmered in the glow of thousands

of bright stars. Jake walked around the small campfire and stood looking down into the flames. Betty and Carlo were sitting cross-legged opposite the fire from Jake, Carlo holding a metal cup in his lap. Betty said something, voice low, but Jake couldn't hear what she said.

Looking up from the fire, Jake could see the slight, short figure of Mason standing at the edge of the camp. Mason's back was to the camp; he was looking out across the field. He had been unusually quiet since they had started this journey.

"There she is," said Betty, this time loud enough that Jake could hear.

He turned about and looked up the Road, the dirt surface aglow beneath the starlight. Meara was strolling down the center of the road, her figure similarly luminous. Reaching camp, she stepped up beside Jake. He raised a brow, giving her a questioning look. She shook her head in response.

Once camp had been established, she had insisted on walking a ways further up the Road, wanting to ensure no dangers lay immediately ahead in the dark. This had become a daily ritual of Meara's that Jake had grown accustomed to in their past travels, and that Jake had come to appreciate.

It was nice to know their surroundings when settling in for the evening.

The journey so far had been uneventful, very quiet. They had made good time, walking a constant, steady pace, stopping every few hours for short breaks, a half hour for lunch, stopping each evening at sunset. The countryside remained mostly unchanged; fields of tall grass, occasional lone trees and clusters of brush.

It was the same landscape that Jake had traveled through by bus those summers past, yet it seemed curiously different. On foot, walking the road, it was somehow different than when viewed through the windows of the bus. It had seemed normal back then...

Was it really different now?

Maybe it was Jake that had changed.

He backed away from the fire, took the few steps up onto the road. He stuffed his hands into the pockets of his jacket. He let his eyes adjust, then looked up and down the road.

In those summers past, traveling to the village from the outside world, the old bus would turn off the two lane county highway of the real world and start down this dirt and gravel road. Jake remembered that it took about three hours back then to get to the gates of Serpent's Keep; about a hundred miles.

So... had the outside world still been out there, it would as yet be another several days' journey.

But then, the outside world, *the real world*, wasn't out there. Not any more. This much they knew.

So what would they find? How long before they found it? Where were the boundaries of their world and what lay beyond, if anything?

Meara left the fire and joined Jake. She looked past him and up the road, then the other direction. The shell of stars above set it all near incandescent.

"Is everything all right, sir?" she asked.

"Everything is fine, Meara."

Meara looked up and down the road yet again. "Good," she said softly.

Jake looked side-glance to Meara, half turned and looked out across the field beyond the camp.

"I was just thinking," he said, almost to himself.

Meara leaned a bit nearer.

"Sir?"

"I was thinking of the ledge above the Great Ravine, the ledge that looked down into the ravine."

Jake and Meara had camped that night on the ledge. They had looked down into the ravine as dusk was falling, had seen silhouettes and shadows gliding above the forest blanketing the ravine floor.

That had been the first time that either of them had seen dragons...

"That was a long time ago, sir," said Meara.

And so much has happened since, thought Jake. *Such a long journey.*

"Yes. A very, very long time ago," he said, as if to himself.

This road was that ledge. Up ahead were the silhouettes of dragons.

The main thoroughfare of Serpent's Keep lay in a murky, silvery gray fog; the row of street lamp globes hung in a drifting night mist some twelve feet above the brick surface of the pedestrian street, each lamp a dull, yellowy gold, the hazy glow just reaching the ground.

Sheriff Smith passed beneath one of the street lamps, passed through its cone of light. It was late evening, the village was quiet, its citizens having settled into their homes for the night; lit curtained windows shone through the fog, aglow with both electric light and oil lamps.

The sheriff continued his rounds, passing beneath the next lamp; the intersection beyond lay half in shadow, half in light. Reaching the corner, he turned and walked into the dark of the narrow side street. Diffusely lit light fixtures hung on the south walls every few dozen paces.

He reached the west gate guard station at the end of the street. The woman standing civilian watch stepped out of the guard shack, stood before the heavy wooden gate and gave a nod to Sheriff Smith.

"Good evening, Sheriff," she said.

"Rebecca." Sheriff Smith acknowledged the young woman, then looked past her to the gate. "How are we doing this evening?"

"All's quiet. Team two checked in a couple of minutes ago."

Several two person teams walked the perimeter on the other side of the wall, a relatively new security measure. The teams stopped at each gate and checked in with the watch on duty.

Sheriff Smith looked from the gate again to Rebecca. "Do you need anything?"

"I'm good."

"Great." The sheriff hesitated, then turned to leave and continue his rounds. "You have a good evening, then."

"Sheriff?" Rebecca called after him.

He turned back, waited.

"Sorry, Sheriff; but..." Rebecca wavered, wore a guilty expression. "Have you heard anything from the Farm?"

Rebecca's kid brother was a member of the team that had been sent to help defend the Farm, should it be necessary. Sheriff Smith understood, and tried to appear supportive, but there really was very little that he could say to reassure her.

"No, ma'am. It's really too soon."

"Right, right," mumbled Rebecca. "You're right."

"You hang in there, Rebecca."

"Yes. I'll do my best."

Sheriff Smith took a step back toward her.

"Rebecca, I believe absolutely that Ethan will be back here giving me headaches in no time."

Rebecca managed a smile. "I'm sure you're right."

"I wouldn't say it if I didn't believe it."

"Thank you, Sheriff," she said after a long pause.

Sheriff Smith gave a comfortable smile in response, stepped back and turned to walk the narrow dark side street back to the main thoroughfare.

He had the other gates to visit this evening.

TahLyn sat in the heart of the large clearing, staring up into the night. The splay of stars were unfamiliar to her. Such had been the case each night of this journey.

The clearing they had settled into for the night was well off the Dark Path, enclosed on three sides by tall brush. The Lynhaur dragon sat a few yards from TahLyn, a dark shadow in the shadows, wrapped within its wings against the cool of the night. The two large Thrauhm of the team were squatting at opposite sides of the clearing, facing outward; they were asleep and yet not asleep, ready to respond to any threat that might come near.

TahLyn let her eyes close. She listened to the dull whisper of white noise around her. She let out a long, slow breath, the wide nostrils of her snout expanding. She let her thoughts drift back along their journey so far, for the most part uneventful, to where they now found themselves.

They were still several days from the farthest point they had previously reached along the Dark Path, and yet TahLyn had already noted differences from their previous journeys. There were the changing shell of stars each night, yes, but also milestones that she had noted previously were no longer there, new landmarks taking their place. On any other trip out they would be investigating each of these changes, but not on this journey. This journey had but one purpose, and TahLyn refused to be distracted by the admittedly curious alterations to the Dark Path.

A rustling, hollow swishing sound reached into TahLyn's thoughts, drifted into her thoughts. Her eyes opened; she gazed about.

All was still. She listened. There was only silence, in the clearing and beyond.

Movement then...

The Lynhaur opened its wings to the rustling of wing against body, stretched them out, then drew them in, folded them back against the sides of its body.

Silence again...

TahLyn half-turned her head and looked over at the two Thrauhm. One sat with eyes closed, the other was calmly watching TahLyn.

TahLyn gave a very brief, short nod.

The heavyset Thrauhm, mollified, heaved a long, slow breath and closed its eyes, ready to respond as needed.

TahLyn shifted about, looked about, looked beyond the clearing. The night was so very still, so very quiet. There was not even so much as a breeze to brush across the grass, to push through the surrounding brush.

Glancing above, the thousands of unfamiliar stars splashed across the jet-black night sky, painted a silvery glow over the landscape.

TahLyn returned her attention to her companions in the clearing. Their presence comforted her. She shifted again and settled again into her sleep position.

And yet… she was not ready to sleep.

She would rest, then; that, at least.

She let her eyes slowly close, let her thoughts wander where they would.

The night passed.

Chapter Nine

Master Peter and his traveling companions had been walking through the forest since just after dawn. The midmorning air was cool, the overcast gray sky visible now and then through the leaves and branches of the forest canopy above them. There was no sign of the sun.

Up ahead, the young monk leading the way stopped, looked back to the others. He waited then for Peter and John to catch up to him.

"What do you have?" asked Peter.

The young monk indicated ahead of them.

Just visible through the trees, several hundred feet ahead, was the front of a building, its stone steps leading up to a set of heavy doors.

"The North Temple," said John.

"It would appear so," said Peter. He gave the young monk a pat on the shoulder and moved out ahead, leading the way.

They stepped out of the trees as a group. As they did, two figures came through the temple doors and stood at the top of steps. They were dressed in monk robes, but robes different than those of Peter and his temple; different in style and color. Theirs were dark green, with narrow collars and tailored hems.

"The Lost Monks," Peter said quietly, calmly. When one of the younger companions gave him a curious look, he indicated those standing at the top of the steps. "The robes," he said. *The robes of the Ancient Monks.*

Peter moved forward and stood at the foot of the steps.

"We have traveled a long way," he said.

"So you have," said one of the two standing at the top of the steps. "The Serpent's Keep Temple."

"We are occasionally referred to as such. My name is Peter."

The monk let his gaze drift from one to another of the arrivals, returning then to Peter.

"I am August, abbot of this sanctuary." He indicated the monk standing beside him. "My associate, Brother Tarrant."

"The North Temple," said John.

August looked to John, initially curious, then in understanding.

"We have been alone for a very long time," he said then.

"The Lost Monks."

"The Ancient Monks," said the young monk standing beside John.

Master August again appeared curious, wrinkling a brow, questioning, but said nothing.

"If I might," said Peter. "The scrolls describe the disappearance of the distant North Temple long before the division of the Outland and the scattering of the temples, which itself was a very long time ago."

"I see." August considered, then turned and indicated the sanctuary's front doors behind him. "Please. I would like to hear more."

Meara stopped. Jake and Mason were far ahead along the Road, walking at an easy pace. Betty and Carlo, trudging several steps behind Meara, moved up beside her, said nothing, waited.

Meara pulled her canteen out of its holster, twisted off the cap and took a swallow. She looked about at their surroundings.

The landscape had changed over the last few days. The fields to either side were dusty, barren; there were occasional clumps of vegetation scattered about, brown with brown leaves and bare branches.

The air was dry, warm. The sun was sitting low on the horizon.

Meara noticed then that Jake and Mason had stopped and were looking back at them. She closed her canteen and returned it to the holster on her hip, looked side-glance to Betty and Carlo.

Carlo lifted a brow. *Lead the way...*

As they drew near Jake and Mason, Meara saw a large, boxy silhouette a few hundred yards beyond. Something was sitting alongside the road; pre-dusk shadows were swathed over the object and the desolate landscape stretching away to either side of the road.

"What is that?" she asked.

"Let's find out," said Jake. He led the way then, and they continued down the center of the road. After a few dozen yards the boxy silhouette took on the shape of an old bus. It looked very much like the bus that Meara had occasionally seen pulling up outside the village's main gate.

They reached the vehicle. Meara looked from the bus to Jake.

Jake had a strange, puzzled look on his face.

Mason lifted a hand and rested it on the side of the bus, as if to make sure that it was really there.

Jake moved to the door, hesitated and then pushed it open. He gave one tentative look to Meara before climbing inside.

"Mason?" asked Meara, looking over at the little man.

Mason lowered his hand, took a step back and slowly shook his head. Meara took several steps back then and took it all in; at the bus parked alongside the Road, at their desolate surroundings.

The bus appeared to be abandoned. More than abandoned; it looked to be long abandoned. It was covered in years of dust and dirt, the windows now opaque with gray grime. The tires, the rubber faded gray, were near flat, several sitting on their rims.

Jake reappeared in the open door. He looked all the more bewildered.

"Nothing," he said. "Empty."

"Is it…?" asked Meara.

Jake stepped down, stepped away from the bus.

"Oh, yes," he said. "It's the bus."

"Of course it is," grumbled Mason.

It was the same bus that Jake had taken each and every time he had traveled from the outside world to Serpent's Keep.

"How can that be?" she asked. "This bus has been here a long time."

"I know."

"A very long time, Jacob Quigley," said Mason.

"I know." Jake turned about, gave the old bus a long, careful study. "I was on this very bus a couple of years ago."

"What are you saying?" asked Betty, asked Carlo, at almost the same time.

"It's been sittin' here a lot longer than a couple of years, sir," said Meara.

"I know."

Mason frowned, pursed his lips, gave another even darker frown; he looked at the bus through bushy brows. "Time's different out here," he grumbled.

Jake thought about that for a long moment, looked back then down the Road, back the way they had come: to the Outland, to the village of Serpent's Keep.

"Or it's different back there," he said, tentatively. *It's us existing out of time...*

Meara glanced up at the sky, looked to the west. The sun was sitting low on the horizon.

"It'll be dark soon," she said. "Maybe we should stop for the day."

"I'd rather not," said Jake firmly. He started down the Road, leaving the others to follow.

"All right," Meara mumbled.

§

Charles Victor was kneeling behind the stack of empty wooden crates, leaning around and peering around the crates enough to be able to see what was unfolding in the open compound area in the center of the farm. The farm managers shotgun was leaning against the boxes beside him.

Eighteen year old Ethan was kneeling beside him. He had a slight frame, wore loose-fitting shirt and pants. He was looking at Charles Victor's bloody shirt.

"Are you all right?" he asked.

"Don't you worry about me, Ethan," said Charles. The wound in his side had been bound, the bleeding stopped. He shifted his weight from his left knee to his right, taking the pressure off his injured side.

He watched as a group of ten to twelve raiders worked their way into the farm's compound. Several of the raiders confronted a handful of farm defenders head-on as other bandits pushed still other defenders back into the main barn. The direct hand-to-hand lasted only a few moments before the fights broke up and the defenders retreated into one of the smaller barns.

Charles slid back behind the crates, squatted fully onto his haunches. He wore a dark, fretful frown.

"Mr. Victor?" asked Ethan.

Charles shook his head. It was all but done. No one had been killed as yet, so far as he could tell, but the farm was all but lost, and Charles didn't know what would be coming next.

What do they want beyond produce? Is this all for a few potatoes and onions?

He was startled at the sound of three gunshots. He pushed off his haunches and onto a knee, peered again around the stack of crates.

There was no movement in the farm compound, but he could hear struggling going on inside the barns. Briefly then, he saw figures moving behind and between the barns; thin wisps of smoke hovered in the air.

Another group of bandits were meeting with some resistance…

Charles slid back, turned and looked carefully at Ethan.

He's just a kid. What's he doing here?

"Are you up for a jog?" he asked.

"I guess so," said Ethan, no idea where this was going.

"Good. I need you to do something for me."

"Sure, Mr. Victor. Anything."

"Hurry back to the village. As fast as you can."

"Sir?"

"We're all but done here. Get to the sheriff. Let him know what's happening. Give him the numbers. We appreciate the folks that he sent our way, but it isn't near enough. We need help."

"All right." Ethan looked anxiously about. "I can do that."

"I know you can," said Charles. He shifted again, placed a hand on the boy's shoulder. He gave a nod to the south. "Cut across the southwest forty, come out onto the road as far south as you can. Don't stop till you reach the village."

Charles struggled then to his feet, turned and looked around the crates. There was no movement, no sign of the bandits.

"It's all clear, boy," he said over his shoulder. "Go now. Good luck."

"I'll bring back help, sir."

Ethan scrambled to his feet and started across the field. Charles continued to watch for signs of trouble until he was sure the boy had made it safely away. Only then did he reach down and pick up his shotgun, step around the crates and start across the open space between the crates and the nearest farm building.

He would try to reach the defenders that were currently taking on the band of raiders on the other side of the farm, beyond the barns.

TahLyn came upon what looked to be a long-abandoned human campsite. Brush enclosed the clearing, in the center of which was a small circle of stones, the cold ash remains of a campfire.

She lifted her gaze from the tiny fire pit to look beyond the perimeter of brush. Beyond the camp, the vast plain spread out across the landscape in all directions. The purple silhouette of a distant mountain range lay across the horizon; still several days' travel distant.

It was believed the Ancient Guardian lived in a castle in the mountains. TahLyn hoped what lay on the horizon was in fact the home of Aldwyn. She had sent the Lynhaur ahead to see what was to be seen.

She turned to the pair of Thrauhm Jahai. The large dragons waited patiently just beyond the clearing. One, seeing the Bentai Jahai turning to look to them, tilted its head slightly, expectantly, its mouth opening, closing.

"Yes," TahLyn stated. "We have hours remaining to us before night. Let us continue."

Both Thrauhm rose up, readied. They waited.

TahLyn left the clearing and started walking again, continuing in the direction of the mountain range, currently little more than a smudge of silhouette on the horizon. Her Thrauhm traveling companions followed quietly behind.

Tobias was sitting on a fallen tree lying alongside the trail. He was eating a late lunch, munching on dried fruit and jerky. The forest was very thick here. The trail before him looked to be seldom used, was little more than an animal trail, and was used by very few animals at that.

Tobias had left the site of the temple ruin several days before, starting out in the morning after bidding farewell to Khol. He had grown rather close to the Bentai during their travels and their time together at the temple ruin. He hoped to see him again before too long, and looked forward to checking in on the work being done to create a permanent presence at the ruin site. Several different species of dragon continued to trickle in a few at time.

He estimated that he had another five or six days of rations, including nuts and cheese, dried fruit and jerky. Making a side trip on his way home may not have been the best idea, as it put him at least another week from Serpent's Keep, but his curiosity had gotten the best of him. He had never been to that region of the Outland, as it was a newly reunited section, and he wanted to give it a quick visit. On his way back now, he had yet to reach familiar territory.

He picked up his canteen, took a long swallow of water. He checked to see how much he had left. He would need to find a water source soon.

He closed the canteen and set it on the log beside him, then leaned his head back and let what sunlight that managed to reach through the canopy warm his face. It was early afternoon. He should be starting out again soon, as he had another four or five hours of daylight.

Just another five minutes...

There was a sound then, some yards distant, reaching through the trees.

Someone or something was traveling along the narrow trail; a number of footfalls, the occasional pushing aside of branches of brush bordering the trail, occasional deep grumblings and grunts.

There was more than one of them, then; quite a few more. And they were coming in his direction.

Tobias waited. Whoever they were, whatever was coming, they would be here soon enough and threat or no, there was little that he could do about it now.

He reached down and picked up his canteen as he watched the trail, barely visible amidst the thick, encroaching brush. He unscrewed the cap, took another swallow. He held the canteen in his lap.

He would do his best to appear unconcerned, even indifferent, to what might be coming.

A dragon appeared then, working his way along the trail; it was a young Bentai, easily maneuvering his way through the overhanging and encroaching brush. Following behind him walked a large Thrauhm Jahai. The Thrauhm had to push aside branches and thick brush to follow.

Tobias could just see other Jahai following behind the Thrauhm; at least one more Bentai and perhaps several other species.

The lead Jahai stopped a few paces from Tobias, warily eyeing the human. The Thrauhm hovered behind the Bentai, towering above the smaller Jahai, watching the human.

Tobias calmly took a swallow of water from his canteen.

"Hello friend," he said then. He set the canteen on the log beside him. He stood, gave a bow of welcome.

The Bentai appeared uncertain at this, a human making a Jahai gesture. Behind him, the Thrauhm lifted its head high, looked down from on high.

Tobias noted that the dragons further back along the trail were doing their best to peer around the larger dragon, struggling to see what was happening.

"Human," the lead Jahai stated.

"That I am," said Tobias. "I am Tobias Quigley."

The Bentai tilted his head, taking in the unfamiliar words of the human, saying nothing.

Hmm, thought Tobias. *Not so impressed.*

"You have traveled far?" he asked.

"Far," said the Bentai. It looked left, looked right, looked again to the human. "We were in web. We were in thread. Bad then. Something bad. We were in gray land, long time. Empty land. Long time. Very long time."

Since the time of the closing, thought Tobias. *A very long time, indeed.*

"I am pleased that you survived such a difficult ordeal, friend," said Tobias.

"We were there," said the Bentai, flatly. "Now we are here."

"You are strong Jahai," said Tobias.

The Jahai looked again from side to side. He tilted his head to look intently at the human.

"Where is *here*, Tobias Quigley?" asked the Bentai.

"Ah," said Tobias. He stepped back, leaned back against the fallen log. "That may take a bit of telling, friend."

Chapter Ten

Jake was standing the last watch. He was out on the Road, the overnight campsite just a few yards off the road. It was early morning, pre-dawn. There had been very little cooling overnight and it looked to be another warm day on the way. Such had been the case the day before, and the day before that. The increasingly barren terrain they were traveling through seemed to reflect the warm, dry weather.

This was not the landscape that Jake remembered from his bus trips to the village, and yet the Road continued before them. They had now traveled far beyond the reach of the last team that Sheriff Smith had sent out.

What was out there? What lay ahead?

There was stirring in the camp. Glancing back, Jake saw that Meara was moving about under her light blanket, just pushing it off. She sat up.

It was quite warm...

Jake again focused his attention outward, then up the Road. The stars had disappeared and the sky was black; the eastern horizon had yet to show any hint of sunrise, leaving the dirt road in darkness. Across the road, the field lay empty and black.

Meara walked over and stood beside Jake.

"Morning," she said quietly, careful not to wake the others.

"Meara," said Jake. "What are you doing up so early?"

"It's too hot to sleep."

Jake agreed. He had in fact started his watch period early, unable to sleep.

He looked back to the others in the camp. They were little more than bundles of shadow encircling the remains of the dinner fire, now only ash.

"That it is," he managed to say, before turning again to look up and down the road.

"You've been awfully quiet the last few days, sir," said Meara. "Is anything wrong?"

Jake had to think about that. Perhaps she was right. He supposed he had been distant of late.

"Most everything, I expect."

"I see. So, nothing specific then…" said Meara, managing a smile.

"Nah," Jake said, shrugging. "Just… it's a lot to take in."

"A lot of questions, and not many answers," agreed Meara.

"You see that too, then."

"Kinda obvious."

Jake said nothing. He noticed the hint of color beginning to form along the distant eastern horizon. Looking about, the black was just beginning to gray; not much, but a little.

"Sir?" Meara prompted.

Jake looked side-glance to Meara, then away.

"Sir?" Meara asked again. "Sir, are you thinking that Mason is right? You know, that we are out of time? In some kind of time bubble?"

"Some kind," Jake mumbled.

"Yeah," Meara sighed. "I think so too."

Some kind, thought Jake. *Outside of the rest of the universe... doesn't that put us out of time? Doesn't that put us in a bubble?*

But what did that mean? If out of time, *when* were they? What did that mean? Did *when* even mean anything anymore? Was the outside world moving forward without them? Was time in the Outland moving at all? Was it static?

Geez...

The discovery of the bus had changed everything, and yet had changed nothing. They knew that the world outside had disappeared, that the Outland was alone. The question of time may have complicated things, but so far as day-to-day life in the Outland it meant little.

Jake let out a loud sigh.

Dawn colors began to paint across the eastern horizon.

Dawn. Another day. Time…

Jake spoke while looking up the road, a winding band of black turning a shimmering brownish gray.

"You're not regretting coming along, are you Meara?"

"I expect you know me better than that, sir."

"Expect I do," said Jake. He watched the horizon. He liked to stand the last watch, liked the sunrise.

The world around them quickly lightened then, black to gray to splashes of orange and red and yellow.

"It's a nice change from the Outland," said Meara.

Interesting choice of words, thought Jake. *She gets it. We are no longer in the Outland.*

So, where are we? Not in the Outland, yet not in the outside world.

We are somewhere in between.

He sensed movement behind them, a stirring in the camp.

The others were beginning to wake.

"I should get the coffee going," he said.

Peter followed Brother Tarrant down the narrow hall of the west wing of the North Temple, each of them passing through the dull yellow orbs of light that were formed by the widely spaced lamps. The air was musty and there was the faint taste of lamp oil on the tongue. Back home, in Peter's own temple, they had long ago added ventilation to this hallway and to the east wing hall to help freshen and clean the air.

He might mention the option to
Master August if the subject ever
presented itself and Peter could do so
without seeming to offend. In their
time here Peter had found that while
August was hospitable and cordial, he
was quick to become defensive, and
for what Peter thought to be the
most minor of reasons.

Despite this, and despite their very
different personalities, Peter liked the
abbot and they got along well
enough. Master August was a pleasant
host and Peter was enjoying his time
at the North Temple. Their exchange
of information was ongoing, with
unexpected discoveries coming daily,
many having to do with their
divergent histories since the
disappearance of the North Temple.
So, while Peter looked forward to
returning home, he had not yet set a
date to depart.

Brother Tarrant opened the door
near the end of the hall. Peter
followed him through and into the

North Temple's library. He stood in the middle of the room, lit by half a dozen lamps placed strategically about the library. It was very similar to the library back home, with the walls lined floor to ceiling with shelves filled with old books, and a section of diamond-shaped honeycomb shelves filled with scroll tubes. In some way that Peter couldn't point to, this library had an even stronger air of antiquity than their own. It smelled of old paper and oiled papyrus, of book glue and centuries-old wood.

But then so did the library back home. So what was it? There was something different about this library, something that spoke to Peter of the distant past.

He hoped that before he left here that he would be able hear what it was trying to tell him.

Master August approached from the far end of the room with several scroll tubes tucked under his arm.

"Ah, there you are Peter," he said. He gave a smile to Tarrant. "Thank you, Tarrant. That will be all."

Tarrant nodded and backed away, turned about and left the room, closing the door behind him. August walked to a table that was cluttered with papers, folders and a large ceramic mug. A pole lamp stood directly beside the table. He set the scroll tubes onto the table and dropped himself into one of two chairs. He scooted the chair forward and picked up the mug, took a long swallow from the contents and watched Peter sit in the chair opposite.

"Your morning goes well?" asked August.

"I've been meditating in the garden," said Peter. "It was quite pleasant."

"Yes. One of my favorite places to go when I'm seeking to quiet my thoughts and feed my soul."

"I can certainly understand why it would be so." Peter leaned forward, placed his forearms on the table and clasped his hands. "You asked to speak with me."

"That I did, Peter. That I did." August pulled himself nearer the table, moved a few items aside and held the mug between his hands and leaned forward. "I've been assimilating the information that you have provided regarding the network of temples into the information that we have here; the data detailing the temples before our isolation, what information there is following the dispersal of the temples that you have described. I have attempted to mesh that data, if you will, with that of our own history, both before and after our isolation from the other temples, and the facts as we have always understood them."

"Quite the project, I would imagine," said Peter.

"To be sure," August stated evenly. Key to his investigation was the ability to reinterpret what he thought he knew, and importantly the ability to interpret the data that was contained in their scrolls from his newly modified perspective. August found that he had needed to reevaluate all that he thought he knew, to step back and explore the world around him with a different set of eyes.

Brother John stepped out of the garden, followed the walk along the wall of the North Temple's main building. Coming around the corner, he found Master Peter standing at the top of the front steps. Peter appeared to be lost in thought, though he did silently acknowledge John when he climbed the steps and stood beside him.

"Master Peter," said John. "I was told that you were meeting with Master August. I trust it went well."

Peter let his gaze drift across the clearing and above the forest of the

Outland beyond. He took a moment to gather his thoughts.

"We have always been rather pretentious when it comes to our temple," he said at last. "In relation to the other sanctuaries. Have we not?"

"I haven't given it much thought, really," said John, unsettled by the question. "Until quite recently, we were alone."

"On our own, perhaps, but not alone. We knew that our brethren were out there, somewhere."

"I suppose that is so," John said, his thoughts jumbled. "That happened long before my time."

"Hmm," Peter mumbled. "Mine, as well."

"Sir?"

"Nonetheless..." said Peter, his own thoughts drifting.

"Yes sir..."

They stood silent for several very long moments then. It was late afternoon, the air was warm and still. John thought he saw movement in the trees, small animals moving about in the shadows; creatures were just beginning to move about after a long day of slumber.

"We were apart from one another for far too long," sighed Peter.

"We were, sir."

Peter looked briefly at John, forward again.

"Ours was not the original temple," he said.

"Sir?" John had always thought the temples had been built at about the same time, when he thought about it at all. Looking at them now, they were certainly designed and constructed similarly.

"If there was what one would call a primary sanctuary, it was this one," said Peter. "The North Temple."

"It does seem to stand apart from the others," said John.

"Hmm," sighed Peter. "Knocks us down a peg, doesn't it?"

"I don't understand."

Peter managed something between a grin and a smirk. He had always felt his own temple to be special. After all, there was Serpent's Gate, primary to the outworld gates, literally at their front steps.

Nothing but happenstance, as it turned out. The purpose of the temples had been to bear witness to the good and the bad of humankind, with but a tenuous relationship to the gates.

"August believes there is a strong connection between the North Temple and the Ancient Guardian," said Peter.

Of course he does... thought John.

"And is there?" he asked.

"Maybe," shrugged Peter. "Maybe it has something to do with the North Temple disappearing all those years ago; long before the division of the Outland."

"I see," said John.

"Really?" Peter looked to John, again to the sky hovering above the Outland. "I wish I did."

Sheriff Smith's footfalls sounded down the narrow side road deep into the north end of the village. He stopped at an unmarked door located midway along the long brick wall that spanned the length of the road and the row of buildings behind it.

He hesitated a moment, as if gathering up the courage to face what waited for him inside. He reached out then, opened the door and entered the Adventurer's Guild.

The front foyer was a small room; off-white colored walls, gray carpet, soft lighting. A tall, elderly man in conservative slacks and jacket stood behind a high counter of dark wood. A set of double doors in the wall beside and behind the counter stood slightly ajar. The low rumbling of a dozen quiet conversations could be heard coming from beyond the doors.

"Good evening, Sheriff Smith," the man behind the counter said softly, his tone formal.

"Good evening, Broderick." The sheriff stood facing the doors, a hand resting on the countertop beside him.

Broderick looked to the doors, then to the sheriff.

"They appear to be friendly enough this evening, sheriff," he said reassuringly.

"Good to hear." Sheriff Smith knew everyone in the room. He knew everyone in the village.

He just didn't like speaking to a crowd.

To it, then...

He stepped through the doors and entered the guild's main hall. It was a spacious room, though not overly large. There were half a dozen round tables scattered about the floor, with a handful of smaller tables set along the walls and interspersed with high-backed chairs. This evening, all the tables and chairs were occupied.

Most of the conversations stopped as Sheriff Smith crossed the room, moving between the tables. He placed a hand on one shoulder and another, mumbling an occasional 'hello' or a 'good evening'.

Reaching the far wall, he turned about and faced the room. Ethan, the young man that had brought Sheriff Smith the news from the Farm, was sitting at a nearby wall table with his sister Rebecca.

The sheriff looked from Ethan to the room at large.

"Thank you for coming, everyone," he said. "I won't take too much of your time."

He paused briefly as another person came into the room. It was Wanda, the captain of the Civilian Watch. She gave an apologetic smile and then stood with her back against the wall beside the double doors, folded her arms across her chest.

Sheriff Smith gave her a nod of welcome, looked again about the room, let the room fall quiet. All eyes fell on him; all in the room grew expectant.

"You all know what's happened at the Farm," he said then. He looked over to Ethan, gave him an affable smile, turned again to the room, his expression again growing dark. "I won't go into details, beyond to say that the severity of the attack is beyond appalling."

"Has anyone been killed?" asked a middle-aged woman. Sheriff Smith knew that her son had been one of those sent to help defend the Farm.

"I do not believe so," he answered. He glanced to Ethan, who gave only the slightest shake of the head. He turned back to the woman. "Injuries, to be sure, but we do not believe anyone has been killed."

"What now?" asked a man sitting at another table.

"That is why I have asked you all here." Sheriff Smith stepped near Ethan and his sister. He placed a hand on Ethan's shoulder, took a few moments to look at each person in the room. "We have been asked to provide further assistance. We will provide that assistance."

"Sending more out to the Farm?" asked the man.

"That's right."

A number of people began talking at once. The sheriff heard a few rumblings of concern about leaving the village undefended.

"Hold on, folks." Sheriff Smith stepped away from Ethan, held up his hand. "A moment, please."

He waited for the loud din to fall to low grumblings. He indicated Wanda then, who was still standing at the back of the room.

"Wanda will be meeting with her team leaders in the morning to organize additional enhancements to the village defenses. I can assure you we will be well prepared for any eventuality."

"We thought that with the Farm," came from one in the crowd.

"That's true enough," admitted the Sheriff. "I take responsibility for that."

"Not yours alone, Sheriff," said another. "It's on all of us."

"I appreciate that, but it was my call." The sheriff's expression brokered no argument. "Now. The situation at the farm will be resolved. And the village is another matter entirely."

"That it is," came from one in the crowd.

"We are prepared for any eventually," the sheriff stated again, firmly.

A return of the grumblings then, some of doubt, others of hesitant acceptance; most agreed.

"In the meantime," Sheriff Smith continued, urging quiet. "Wanda has designated a team leader from the guard who is at this moment organizing the team that will be heading to the Farm at first light."

He took another few moments to look directly at the men, women and young people in the room. He expected that most everyone in the room, most everyone in the village, would be asked to volunteer to defend the village. He also fully expected that most, if not all, would step forward and accept.

"We will get through this," he said. He paused then, gave a general nod to all. "Together."

And with that the meeting began to break up. Wanda caught the attention of several in the room, led them out of the guild hall. Most everyone else remained, however, and the hall filled with the growing rumble of a dozen conversations.

The sheriff caught Ethan's attention and the young man came over, his sister Rebecca right beside him.

"How are you feeling, Ethan?" asked the sheriff.

"I'm fine, Sheriff. Just fine."

"Good to hear. Listen, I know you're anxious to get back to the Farm, but I have something else in mind for you."

"Sure, Sheriff," said Ethan. "Whatever you need."

Rebecca looked on with concern. She was glad that Ethan wouldn't be going back to the Farm, but she was apprehensive about what the sheriff was going to ask of her brother.

"I appreciate that, Ethan," said the sheriff. "So, here it is. I would really like for you to make a trip out to the Temple. I need you to tell Master Peter what's happened."

"Sheriff?" asked Ethan.

"Trust me," said the sheriff. "It's important that he knows what's going on. Can you do that for me?"

"Are you worried they might attack the Temple?" asked Rebecca.

"That is certainly a possibility," said Smith. "They should be prepared for that, but actually... Master Peter might be able to offer some assistance."

"Really?" asked Rebecca. *What can a bunch of monks do?* she wondered to herself.

"Really," said the sheriff. "You would be surprised."

"Okay, Sheriff," said Ethan. "Should I leave now?"

"Best not just yet. It'll be dark before long." Sheriff Smith placed a hand on the young man's shoulder. "The morning will be soon enough."

"Sure, Sheriff. You got it," said Ethan after a long pause. "I'll leave at first light."

Rebecca took a step in the direction of the door, looked from Sheriff Smith to her brother.

"Let's go, Ethan," she said. "If you're gonna be headin' to the Temple tomorrow, there's prep to do."

Ethan gave an uncomfortable grin to the sheriff as he took a shuffling step toward his sister.

"Guess I gotta go, Sheriff."

Sheriff Smith nodded farewell to the young man and watched Ethan and his sister work their way through the still mingling crowd and to the door. Several others followed, though most of those who had attended the meeting remained.

Friends and neighbors, ordinary folks, being asked to do stand up and do extraordinary things.

Sheriff Smith wished he felt as confident about their future as he let on.

Chapter Eleven

The animal trail that had paralleled the road running from the Farm to the village turned sharply and emptied onto the road itself. Janice stopped, took a step back from the road. From here she could see the Serpent's Keep wall and the north gate just a few hundred yards further south.

Thomas, the man that Janice most relied on to handle the security of their Rhetani temple, stepped up behind her and looked past her. He moved then beside her, studied the empty road north and then south. He watched as a pair of guards followed the village wall, passed the gate. They continued on along the wall until they disappeared from his view.

"All's quiet," he said, looking again north up the road. They had witnessed a group of villagers from Serpent's Keep traveling the road an hour or so after dawn, heading for the Farm. Other than that, they had seen no one since they left the assault team encampment several hours northwest.

Janice gave a casual glance up at the sky and sun, back behind them into the woods.

They should probably move back further off the road.

She looked up at the sky again, checked the sun's location again: it was about an hour till midday. The rest of her team would be breaking camp soon and starting their way.

"Let's find a spot to bivouac," she said. "Lunch in an hour."

Thomas placed a hand on Janice's arm, gently pulled them both back further into the trees, further from the road. Alert now, Janice silently complied.

They held silent and motionless.

A long minute later Tobias passed by, walking the road at an easy pace, staff in hand, heading to the village's North Gate.

The North Gate was unique among the village gates in that it had a smaller door set into the larger double gate that was used only when the produce wagons needed wider passage on their way to or from the Farm. Tobias approached and pulled on a rope hanging from a hook and running through a hole in the wall.

He waited.

Several moments passed before the guard standing watch on the other side of the gate called out to him.

"Who calls?"

"Tobias Quigley."

Another moment, then Tobias heard the sound of the heavy crossbar sliding aside. The smaller gate opened; a young man took two steps back and waited. Tobias stepped through the gate.

"Welcome home, Master Quigley," said the guard.

"Thank you, young man. It is good to be home." Tobias stepped past the guard and continued into the village.

The main thoroughfare that he walked and the side streets that he passed were strangely quiet, all but empty. Looking into the market plaza, he noted that most of the booths were closed; the three or four patrons that he saw wandering the marketplace for the most part passed the handful of open booths without stopping.

He passed no one while walking the thoroughfare down the center of the village. Indoor lighting shone through the window of the café, but there was no sign of movement within. On the other side of the way, the window shutter of the sheriff's office was open.

Tobias continued on to the side road of his estate, followed the estate's fence to the wrought-iron gate. Overhanging trees put the street and the estate into shadow. He unzipped the inside pocket of his jacket and brought out his key, unlocked the gate.

Entering the Quigley Mansion, he stood in the middle of the foyer and slipped out of his knapsack. He took a moment to let the soothing atmosphere of home envelope him.

How many times over the years had he come home, stood in that very spot and let this room warm and heal his soul?

Hundreds of times at least...

"Master Quigley. Welcome home, sir." Mr. Griffin was standing at the top of the stairs. He tried his best to maintain a calm decorum as he descended. "It is so good to see you, sir; so very good to see you."

"Thank you, Mr. Griffin. It is good to be home," said Tobias. He raised a brow. "It is, is it not? Good to be home?"

"Sir?"

"I've just had a rather disquieting walk through the village," he said. "What have I missed?"

"That would depend, Master Quigley," said Griffin. "What do you know of recent events?"

"Dear Mr. Griffin. I do miss our little chats."

"As do I, sir," said Mr. Griffin. He went on then to describe the attack on the Farm and the teams that had been sent out to defend it. He noted the sheriff's concern that the village might be next.

The Farm, thought Tobias. If he had taken his normal route home he would have walked right passed the farm. He had instead gone cross country through the woods, coming out onto the road well south of the farm.

He took a moment then to consider. Would bandits have made

such an assault on their own? Uncertain, but if so they would have grabbed what was immediately at hand and then ran. Tobias doubted they would occupy the farm. They weren't farmers, and in any event he didn't believe they would want to take on the wrath of the village what was certain to follow.

Were the Rhetani behind this? Was Janice behind this?

If so, then the village could very well be a target.

"I've no doubt the sheriff has things well in hand," Tobias said. He would need to drop by the sheriff's office.

"I believe you are correct, sir," said Mr. Griffin. "And he has been working closely with the captain of the Watch."

"Good, good." He looked to the archway leading to the kitchen and dining room. "And how is Mrs. Hodges?"

"Quite well, sir. I am expecting her return before lunch."

"Ah, *lunch*. What a lovely word." Tobias picked up his knapsack. "I'll stow my gear and get cleaned up." He took a step toward the staircase, stopped and looked back to Mr. Griffin. "What of my nephew? Causing trouble, I trust?"

"He has come and gone, Master Quigley. Sheriff Smith sent him on a mission of sorts up the Road."

"Really?"

"Following up on some concern of Mason's, I understand."

"Is that so?" Tobias asked thoughtfully, considering. He liked Mason. The man occasionally wandered into the rather unconventional, but he was never to be dismissed outright.

"He left several days ago," said Mr. Griffin. "Young Meara went with him; as did Mason."

"Sounds like fun," he said, continuing on then to the staircase. "Too bad I wasn't here in time to join them."

"Yes sir." Mr. Griffin started then toward the kitchen. "I will let Mrs. Hodges know that you are home the moment she returns."

Charles Victor and four others sat with their backs against the back wall of the main barn. His shirt was caked with dried blood. The others showed similar signs of injuries. All looked exhausted, several appeared defeated.

Not so Charles Victor. His expression remained defiant.

An armed bandit stood silent watch from a safe distance. He and his fellows had successfully taken the Farm, though few of them knew what they were supposed to do with it now that they had it.

The young man standing guard certainly had no idea.

Would they force these prisoners into farm labor? To what end?

And would they be able to hold onto the farm? Wouldn't the village try to take it back?

Why don't we just load up a wagon with some food and get out of here?

Another of the bandits came around the corner and stood beside the guard. He leaned in and asked the guard a question. In answer, the guard nodded in Charles' direction.

The bandit stepped forward and stood before Charles.

"You run this place?" he asked harshly.

"I'm the manager," said Charles.

"Come on." The bandit took a step back and waited, his weapon at the ready.

Charles clambered slowly to his feet, walked where the bandit indicated, the bandit following two steps behind. He was led around to the front of the barn, the large doors standing open, to where the man Charles thought to be the leader of the bandits waited.

"Here he is, Captain," said the bandit escort.

Captain gave little acknowledgement. He was quietly taking in the view that was spread out before him. The Farm was a well maintained, well managed facility; a handful of beautiful barns, assorted smaller buildings, a small home, and sprawling fields reaching out in all directions from the heart of the farm.

"A nice place you have here," said Captain, not deigning to look at his prisoner.

"Thanks," Charles grumbled. "What do you want?"

Captain did smile then, glancing briefly at Charles before returning his gaze to their surroundings.

"It looks like I have what I want, my man. Don't you think?"

"You don't strike me as a farmer."

"No," Captain smirked. "No, I suppose not."

"So then, you've gone to a lot of trouble to steal a few potatoes."

"Oh, I've never been a big fan of potatoes," said Captain. He smiled. There was something menacing in that expression; but then Captain was well practiced. He knew how to work it. He was good at it.

He hesitated just the right amount of time, then took a step away from the barn. He took another step. Folding his arms, he spoke calmly over his shoulder to Charles.

"How long you figure?" he wondered aloud. "Before we see something more coming up that road?"

"I couldn't say," said Charles. "What do you want from me?"

Another smirk from Captain.

"You mean... now?"

"Why did you ask for me? Certainly not just to revel in your victory."

"Certainly not, sir." Captain turned about and faced Charles Victor. He considered, gave a half turn of the head and a slight nod. "One might consider the events here to be mere distraction. The lady certainly does."

"The lady," Charles stated matter-of-factly.

"Yes. Bit of a know-it-all, really. I don't much care for her." Captain looked briefly about, then directly at Charles. "This is her bit, you know. We thought it might be fun."

"You're having a good time, then."

"No, not really," said Captain with a shrug. "The spoils should be good. Then there's the other. The rewards."

"The other," Charles stated. "Of course."

Captain grinned. "Yeah."

A young woman in faded pants and shirt, blood on one of the sleeves, came around the corner of the barn. She stopped briefly beside the man that had escorted Charles to their leader; she whispered something and then stepped up beside Captain. Captain leaned in, listened a few moments.

He pulled back, a sign of dismissal. The young woman departed.

"Ah, so..." Captain said to Charles, then indicated Charles' escort. "The gentleman here will return you to your friends. We will have to pick this up again later."

"Problem?" asked Charles, raising a single brow.

Captain only grinned at Charles snide insinuation.

"It is what I live for," he said, almost cheerily.

The escort moved into position, frowned and silently ordered Charles to move out ahead of him.

The world around TahLyn and her companions was flat and dry, mostly desolate with occasional islands of gray vegetation. The sky overhead was a cloudless, dull, dusky gray. It never changed, never growing darker, nor brighter. There was no sound, no wind, no movement but for TahLyn and her two Thrauhm dragon companions walking across the barren landscape. The Lynhaur had again been sent out ahead, had been gone most of the morning.

They came upon a small cluster of scraggily shrubs and TahLyn stopped for a short break. The two overlarge Thrauhm settled onto their haunches a few yards away, looked indifferently about them and patiently waited.

The days and nights to now had passed relatively uneventfully. They had travelled terrains of forest, of rolling hills of yellow grass, of barren landscape, journeying ever onward, ever hopeful, now far beyond the farthest reaches of their previous journeys on the Dark Path.

One of the Thrauhm rose up then, took two awkward steps and pushed his great head forward, half-turned his head, eyed the sky in the distance.

TahLyn turned about, looked up into the sky to where her companion was indicating.

A silhouette was set against the pale blue; distant, very distant, but slowly coming ever closer.

Though there was never any real doubt, it was another minute before the silhouette could be recognized as their Lynhaur companion; another minute still before it was circling above them, slowly descending. It finally landed half a dozen long strides from TahLyn.

"I am pleased at your safe return," said TahLyn. "What have you for us?"

"I bring news," said the Lynhaur. It took three short steps, pulling its wings back firmly against its body.

"How so, friend?"

"Mountains," said the flying dragon. "High mountains. Much high. Fill horizon."

"Yes?" urged TahLyn. The Ancient Guardian dwelled in just such a mountain range.

"Saw castle in mountains. Castle. Castle," the Lynhaur stated.

TahLyn stepped forward, stepped around the Lynhaur. She looked to the horizon. Whatever lay ahead was as yet just a smudge of purple silhouette on the horizon, but now she knew, knew for certain, that it was there.

The Dark Path would take them to the Ancient Guardian.

TahLyn spoke then without turning to her companions.

"We have hours yet before night descends." She started forward. "Let us continue."

Chapter Twelve

After the evening meal, Master Peter returned to his sleeping cell to pack up his few belongings in preparation of their early morning departure from the North Temple. Peter and his companions would be leaving before dawn.

They had talked just that morning about possibly starting for home in another two or three days. They had actually begun making plans, then just hours later Brother Tarrant returned from another of his excursions into the Outland with news of bandit activity in the south. Tarrant and his team had been out a number of times since the reintegration of the Outland and such observations were growing more frequent. Tarrant also reported having met with a group of travelers on this latest jaunt. They described to him what sounded to be organized attacks on large groups and several permanent establishments, which was something new for the bandits. And their attacks were growing more brazen and more violent.

While there had been no mention of an immediate threat to their home temple, Master Peter and Brother John were both anxious to get back, just in case. Their sanctuary was always ready for possible assaults, had been since the temples were first established, but with this latest news they weren't comfortable with not being there.

They needed to get home.

Brother John appeared at the open door of Peter's cell.

"Master Peter."

"John." Peter closed his pack. "Anything wrong?"

"I'm just about to go out for my evening walk. Would you like to join me?"

"Thank you, no," said Peter. "There will be plenty of that come tomorrow."

John chose not to remind Master Peter that an evening walk really had nothing to do with walking.

"Yes sir," he said. "Very well, I'm off then."

"I'll see you in the morning," said Peter. He lifted his pack and set it against the wall.

"Yes sir. In the morning then." John left Peter and continued down the hall to the foyer. Once outside, he stood at the top of the steps for a moment and took in the evening air. He descended the steps and walked around to the side of the sanctuary and entered the garden. He followed the wide, winding walkways and paths, bordered by flowering shrubs, passing the occasional wood bench set back off the walks. He came up then to one bench that was occupied.

The abbot of the North Temple looked up at the approaching monk.

"Ah, good evening Brother John," said August.

"Master August," said John with a slight nod. He glanced about them. "It is a pleasant evening. Is it not?"

"That it is." August looked about, again to John. "You will be leaving us, then."

"Come the dawn," said John. "We have much appreciated your hospitality."

"It was our pleasure, I assure you." Master August grew thoughtful, then gave a slight smile. "I admit that we were a bit out of practice, what with our isolation; a most acute isolation, to be sure."

John considered that, finally turned about and sat down beside the abbot. He glanced over at the monk, then ahead, at their surroundings.

"Well, you know, the *Lost Monks* and all," said John. "You've done quite well, really."

"Thank you." Master August had only just begun getting his head around the whole Lost Monks, Ancient Monks story. Seeing their disappearance from the perspective of the other temples, and the inferred connection to the Ancient Guardian, he supposed that it was understandable.

"Odd, you know," said John, almost casually. "The Temples, all together again; the Outland, so much more than I could have imagined."

"No doubt," said August. "Your Temple having stood alone; your temple and the village."

"You know of Serpent's Keep?"

"But of course," said August, quite matter-of-factly. "The home of Tobias Quigley."

§

Janice walked through the main gates and entered Serpent's Keep for the first time in many years. She and her teams had silently worked their way along the village walls, avoiding the side gates and instead assailed the village through the front gates. They easily overwhelmed the sentries that had been posted there, the guards quickly retreating back into the village.

Out ahead of Janice, the two assault teams were rushing up the main thoroughfare, each with its own specific target. She had left the attack on the Farm to Captain and his bandits, while the teams now before her were a mix of both Rhetani and bandits. She would as soon not have involved bandits at all, but as yet there were only a few dozen Rhetani. They couldn't do this on their own.

She turned off the thoroughfare, leaving the teams to their tasks, and entered the park. There was no one there. She followed the walkway across the park and to the gate opposite the Quigley Estate.

Sheriff Smith hovered over the heavy table. He folded his arms and studied the map of the village that was spread across the tabletop. Standing opposite him, Wanda moved a wooden piece an inch across the map, considered, moved it again; she considered again, finally satisfied.

There were seven brown pawns and two red pawns set about on the map.

"Hmm," mumbled the sheriff.

"All is going as anticipated," said the captain of the Civilian Watch.

"Hmm," said the sheriff again. He unfolded his arms, leaned forward and rested his hands on the table. The seven brown pawns, representing groups of villagers, were in position, ready to confront the two smaller attack teams. The village groups were made up of men, women and even older children, virtually the entire population of the village, each led by a member of the Civilian Watch. Wanda was certain they could successfully stand against Janice's assault.

Sheriff Smith was less confident, but he and Wanda had done all they could to prepare. They had even correctly anticipated the assault coming through the main gate.

A young girl, no more than twelve, came into the room. She stood at attention and handed Wanda a folded piece of paper.

"Thank you, Connie," said Wanda. She read the message, gave a smile and a nod to the young girl. "Dismissed."

"Yes ma'am." Connie turned about on her heels and marched out of the room.

Connie took her duties very seriously.

Wanda looked down at the map. She moved one of the red pawns forward, moved two brown pawns directly in front of it.

Sheriff Smith gave long sigh.

"All right, then."

Janice stood across the road from the Quigley Estate.

She recalled the last time she had walked through the wrought-iron gate and up to the heavy door, the garish dragon doorknocker set at eye level. The visit had not gone particularly well. Her argument with Tobias Quigley had been rather heated. Their conflicting views regarding Rhetani philosophy had ended a long relationship.

That had been so very long ago. Back then, the village had been little more than half a dozen buildings scattered about, surrounding Tobias' fenced estate grounds.

She crossed the road now, reached out and checked the gate: locked, as expected. She considered attempting to climbing over but decided against it. She started along the wall surrounding the estate grounds looking for an easier place to hop over than a gate with spikes.

Mr. Griffin stood at the top of the stairs, watched Janice come through the front door and move into the middle of the foyer.

"This way, ma'am," he stated formally. "Master Quigley is expecting you."

"Of course he is," said Janice. She crossed the foyer and climbed the stairs, quietly followed Mr. Griffin down the upstairs hallway.

The deck was much as Janice remembered, though she had only been there a few times. It was enclosed on three sides and open to the west. Tobias Quigley stood near the edge, looking out across the village.

Janice stepped up beside him. Tobias clasped his hands behind his back, continued looking outward. He slowly lifted his gaze from the village to the Outland beyond the west wall.

"Hello, Janice," he said.

Looking down into the streets, Janice saw that they were empty but for a handful of people running from the main thoroughfare into the market plaza at the north end of the village.

"I wasn't sure that I'd find you here, Tobias," she said.

"Oh, I wouldn't miss it."

"Is that so?"

"Absolutely." Tobias turned then to look at Janice for the first time. "Are you here to measure for new curtains?"

"Just checking out my new digs."

"I see." Tobias returned his gaze outward. The streets remained surprisingly quiet. "Honestly, I don't believe things are going as well for you as you think, Janice."

"It's a bit early to come to that conclusion, Tobias."

"Oh, I don't believe so."

Both were quiet for a few moments. Tobias glanced back at the silent Mr. Griffin, who stood waiting near the door. He turned again to look briefly at Janice, then outward, to the village streets and beyond.

"Working with bandits and hooligans, I see," he stated. "I'm disappointed in you, Janice."

"They are but a tool," said Janice. "Nothing more."

"I was always led to believe the Rhetani were more idealistic than that; goals attained through unsavory means are tainted and therefore unworthy."

"Evolving circumstances call for measures that we wouldn't have considered in times past."

Tobias looked directly at Janice. "Has the passage of time changed you so very much?"

"Not really." Janice grew thoughtful, introspective. "Though... I suppose we were quite the wide-eyed romantics back then, we little band of crusaders."

"Perhaps," agreed Tobias, turning to look beyond the village walls. "But it would so appear, each with our own unique perspective on just what it was that we were crusading."

"Hmm," sighed Janice. "And the direction that each would take that crusade. What we would do with it."

"It was not I who fell in with a cult, Janice."

"Cult? Mudslinging now, Tobias?"

"Hurt feelings, Janice? It doesn't become you."

They fell silent yet again. There was some movement in the streets below, an occasional crying out in anger or in strife.

Janice thought it much quieter and calmer than she would have expected, but she managed to hide a growing concern.

"Do you see them much?" she asked. "Our comrades from back then?"

"Now and then," he sighed. "Though not for some time. Jacob, more than I; in his travels."

"Jake. Yes," Janice grumbled. "A bit of an irritant, if you ask me. Where did you find the boy?"

Tobias managed a smile.

"Another life, a different world," he said softly. He lifted a curious brow. "My nephew, don't you know."

"Yeah, so I heard. That would take some explaining."

"Quite."

Another few moments, and then Tobias glanced back to Mr. Griffin, standing near the doorway. He gave the slightest of nods before again looking out across the village.

At that, Mr. Griffin took a step forward, raised a brow to Janice.

"Ma'am," he stated firmly.

Janice looked curiously at Tobias, her expression slowly shifting to confusion.

"It was good to see you, Janice," Tobias said dismissively, his focus remaining outward.

Janice half-turned, looked from Mr. Griffin to Tobias.

"Yes, well," she said. "I will see you again; real soon."

Tobias gave a slight grin, took a long, quiet breath.

"But of course."

Tobias entered the estate's upstairs library. The room was high-ceilinged, with shelved walls, a cherry-wood desk and a leather chair; two high-back chairs sat in one corner beneath a single pole lamp. It wasn't a very large room, and all available space was filled with books.

Stepping up to a section of shelves along the left wall, Tobias reached up and casually pulled at a large book with the title "Creatures in Myth" stenciled on the spine. He heard the catch release, the sound coming from behind the shelves.

He pulled at the shelf section, exposing the access. Stepping through the opening, he felt along the wall on his left and flipped the switch. Three recessed ceiling lights lit up the room; a hallway, twelve feet wide and twenty feet long.

This was Tobias' Hall of Statues.

The six statues stood on short pedestals, three along each side wall, set about five feet apart. They reached nearly as high as the very high ceiling. Each was a unique species of dragon.

The six races of the Jahai.

Tobias walked down the middle of the hall between the statues. He turned left and entered his command center. There was a large, heavy desk near the far end of the room, facing the left wall. The only chair in the room was a large, leather chair behind the desk.

Stepping up to the paneled wall opposite the desk, Tobias pushed a horizontal wood strip to the accompanying sound of another click. He pushed open the hidden door and walked into the supply room.

When he came out a few minutes later, Mr. Griffin was standing beside the desk, waiting.

"Ah. Mr. Griffin." Tobias walked around the desk and dropped into the chair. "How goes the scuffle?"

"The scuffle, sir?"

"The fracas, the confrontation; the battle?"

"Yes, sir. It goes well enough, sir. So I understand. Minimal bloodshed, so I understand."

"Good, good," said Tobias. "I don't mean to make light. Anxiety showing through, I suppose."

"Yes sir."

"And Janice?" asked Tobias, looking up at Mr. Griffin.

"She has departed the estate and grounds."

Tobias could have sworn he saw the hint of a smirk on the face of the stoic Mr. Griffin.

"Good, good," he said again. "I imagine she'll be leaving our fair village soon enough, once reality has had a chance to settle in."

"I would imagine so," agreed Mr. Griffin.

"Which reminds me," said Tobias. "I'll need two week's rations put together."

Mr. Griffin glanced over at the supply room, again to Tobias.

"You are preparing to leave, Master Quigley?"

"That I am, Mr. Griffin; once the dust has settled here."

"Very good," said Mr. Griffin. "I shall advise Mrs. Hodges."

"Thank you." Tobias hesitated then, grew thoughtful. He leaned back in his chair. "The changes out there aren't done just yet, Mr. Griffin. There are the changes that I know are coming, and more yet that I don't. I don't like the not knowing part."

"Yes sir. Of course not, sir." Mr. Griffin took a step back. "I'll see to the rations."

"Thank you, Mr. Griffin."

Tobias watched Mr. Griffin leave the command center, then slowly turned about in his chair. Lost in thought for a minute, he absently glanced up at the old map that was hanging on the wall behind the desk. He gave the map a frown...

Well, that's' going to take some updating...

Jake didn't recognize this stretch of road, hadn't for a number of days now. He was walking well ahead of the others, quietly taking in the solitude of the landscape. The tall grass of the surrounding fields waved gently in the slight breeze.

Far up ahead, what Jake believed to be a wall of trees stretched across the distant horizon. At the moment it was little more than a smear of dark lying across their path.

They walked on. Another hour passed. The silhouette took on the form of a wall of forest. Another half hour and Jake could make out the individual trees.

He slowed his already easy pace. Meara stepped up beside him as he stopped.

"That's the Outland," he stated flatly.

"That's impossible," said Meara. She looked back behind them, along the road they had been traveling for days. "We left the Outland when we left the village."

"Sorry, Meara, but that's the Outland. The North Outland, I'd say."

"But—"

"There. Look." Jake was indicating a spire poking up above the treetops.

"A temple?" Meara asked haltingly.

"North Temple, my guess."

"The Lost Temple? But, how do you figure?"

"The temples are all in the Outland. That includes the North Temple. And I don't see those spires belonging to any of the other temples that we've been to."

"Well, yes sir, but... we've been traveling south," Meara insisted. "Always south. Now we're in the North Outland?"

"Soon will be."

"What, we've gone around the planet?" Meara asked, attempting humor. It fell flat.

"However it's happened, Meara, we're here." Jake gave a nod to the trees. "Serpent's Keep and everything you know is that way."

Meara considered, finally indicated the temple spires, ahead and some way to the right.

"If that's the Lost Temple..."

"Then that's where we need to go."

§

TahLyn continued to work her way up the switchback trail, her two Thrauhm companions trudging very awkwardly along behind her. Rays of sunlight streamed through the trees. The castle was still far above them, intermittently coming into and disappearing from view. The Lynhaur was gliding overhead, circling, watching and waiting.

The afternoon passed quietly; the only sounds were those of the Thrauhms dragging their feet along the trail and their heavy breathing.

Finally then, coming around another switchback, TahLyn suddenly found herself standing directly before the castle. A human stood at the top step, looking down at her, his hands clasped behind his back.

TahLyn moved across to stand at the base of the steps, eyes always on the human. The man was tall, had a thin face, startlingly bright eyes and smile, and long, salt-and-pepper hair. He was wearing loose pants and a long-sleeved shirt, soft shoes.

Aldwyn... the Ancient Guardian...

The Lynhaur dragon glided down from above, dropped down onto the porch a few yards from the Ancient Guardian. It spread its wings, closed them and tucked them along its sides. It shifted sideward then and settled in beside Aldwyn.

The Ancient Guardian acknowledged the Lynhaur, looked again to TahLyn, who continued to stand patiently at the foot of the steps.

"I am Aldwyn", stated the Guardian. "I bid welcome to you all."

"Thank you, Guardian. I am TahLyn." TahLyn indicated the others. "My traveling companions."

"My friends," Aldwyn nodded and smiled.

"We have traveled the Dark Path from the Jahai Village seeking the Ancient Guardian and his guidance."

"My my," said Aldwyn. "I am humbled, to be sure."

The large door behind Aldwyn opened and another human stepped out onto the porch. Corwin, the Ancient Guardian's assistant, was of average height, with pale skin, dark eyes and heavy brows. He was dressed in a heavy brown robe, similar to the garb of other monks that TahLyn had met.

He acknowledged the new arrivals by offering a slight bow, then spoke softly to Aldwyn.

"All is prepared," he said.

"Very good, Corwin," said Aldwyn. He spoke again to TahLyn. "Appropriate accommodations have been prepared for your associates, TahLyn." Aldwyn bowed first to the pair of Thrauhm, then half turned to the Lynhaur and gave a short nod. "Corwin will direct you."

"My pleasure," said Corwin.

"TahLyn," Aldwyn stated then, took a half step back and turned aside. He held out a welcoming hand. "This way, if you would."

Chapter Thirteen

Late afternoon was giving way to another warm dusk; a hint of orange lay across the west horizon at the edge of a near endless world of evergreen and alder and oak, a seemingly endless forest spreading out in all directions from the cluster of granite stones rising up from the forest floor.

Peter was sitting alone atop the Granite Mound, quietly eating his meal, spooning the thick stew from a large bowl. Three of his five traveling companions were sitting nearer the small campfire, finishing up their own early dinners. Another of the monks was standing on a small knob of rock at the far side of the hillock, looking outward.

John walked over to Peter. He sat beside him and set his empty bowl aside. He looked out at the approaching sunset.

"We made good time," he said, filling the silence.

"We did," said Peter. He spooned the last of his stew, sat the bowl beside him.

They could hear their companions behind them, shifting about near the fire pit as they ate their meals, talking quietly among themselves. The atmosphere atop the cluster of rocks was pleasant enough, almost comfortable.

"The weather has changed," John said then. He continued to look to the trees. They were for the most part just below or just at the level of the top of the surrounding canopy. "So still; the air is heavy."

"Hmm," Peter muffled absently. "Humid."

"It's almost like a whole different Outland."

Peter sensed that as well. Still, true as it was, he said nothing.

John brought his knees up, rested his elbows on them and clasped his hands, intertwining his fingers. He glanced back over his shoulder, turned forward again.

"It'll be good to get home."

"It will."

John shifted, adjusted his elbows resting on his knees.

"Master August knows of our temple," he said.

"So I understand."

"And of the village," said John. "And of Tobias Quigley."

"Uh, huh."

"How can that be? The Lost Monks..."

"That I do not know."

John shifted again, leaned further forward, kept his eyes forward."

"Could it be true?" he asked. "A relationship between the Lost Monks and the Ancient Guardian?"

Peter considered.

"Certainly possible," he said at last.

They fell into silence then, the quiet stretching out for half a minute. The sky overhead grew increasingly gray. John mumbled something about there being things to do, then reached for his bowl and stood up. He offered to take Peter's bowl.

Starting away, he suddenly hesitated as he looked outward. He took a halting step nearer the edge.

"Master Peter," he said softly, speaking over his shoulder.

Peter got to his feet and stepped over to stand beside John. He looked in the direction that John had indicated.

A rolling fog was drifting through the forest. It was a thick mist, roiling, rolling, plodding through the trees and encroaching upon the cluster of rocks on which they stood.

"I see," said Peter.

John stepped then to the very edge, looking down into the narrow clearing between trees and rock.

Something there… something in the fog; a darker shadow in the drifting shadows; it appeared to be the silhouette of a man.

"Master Peter?" John urged, not taking his eyes off the shadow.

Peter moved nearer the edge of rock, standing again beside John.

A young man stepped out of the fog. He took the few steps and stood then at the base of the rock wall. He was dressed in canvas pants, a heavy shirt and jacket; a small daypack was strapped to his back.

"That is most interesting," said Peter. He didn't recognize the boy, wondered silently whether he was from Serpent's Keep.

Ethan glanced up, saw the two monks looking down at him. He raised a hand uncertainly, gave a hesitant half wave in greeting.

The pedestrian thoroughfare of Serpent's Keep was eerily still, eerily quiet. The dull, gray evening lay heavily over the village, dampening all sound. A young man wearing a long tan leather coat moved cautiously three paces ahead of Janice, ever watchful for potential threats. None came.

The man turned into an alley. Janice reached the alley moments later and followed him in. The third of the small group, a young woman with long, matted hair and a flannel shirt followed Janice.

Janice had met up with the two only minutes earlier as she was working her way through side streets and back alleys toward the village's east gate and had continued on together.

They turned into a narrow passage and then stepped toward the gate at the end of the way. They approached a pair of guards, members of the civilian watch, who stood at the ready.

"Let us pass," Janice stated coolly.

"I think not, ma'am," said one of the guards.

"It's all done," said Janice. "Do you really want things to get ugly now, when all we want is to leave?"

"It's not our call, ma'am."

Janice looked from one to the other. Both were armed, though they kept their weapons holstered, hands resting casually on the handles. She wasn't armed herself, but her companions were. Both looked ready to act if called upon.

Janice hadn't expected to just walk out, but this looked as though it wasn't going to end well.

So be it. She had no intention of being held prisoner by the likes of simple villagers.

"All right, then." She prepared to signal her companions.

A sound came from behind her... shuffling, movement. Janice hesitated, as did those standing beside her.

"Let them go," came a woman's voice. It was calm but steady.

"Ma'am?" asked one of the guards.

"Open the gate."

"Yes, ma'am." The one guard signaled the other, who moved to open the gate.

Janice glanced back behind her. A woman stood in the center of the alleyway, two others stood behind her; all looked ready to respond as needed.

Janice gave a brief nod to the woman.

Wanda, the head of the civilian watch, did not respond. Her gaze was sharp, her expression firm, almost severe.

Whatever... thought Janice. She turned forward again. The gate was opening, the guards moving to either side. They gave her a cold look as they waited.

Janice stepped forward, walked between them; she ignored them as she stepped through the gate and out of the village, her companions following.

Wanda watched them leave. She gave a sharp nod to the guards. One closed the gate, the other lifted to wood crossbar into place.

A dark frown then, Wanda turned about and walked between the two watch members standing with her and left the alley.

Jake stood in the center of the Road, his hands stuffed into his jacket pockets. He was looking ahead at the wall of trees, the stand another thousand yards further on. The road ended at the forest wall. The sun had set just minutes earlier and the west horizon was painted in quickly fading orange. The landscape to either side of the dirt road lay in low, scrubby grass and weeds.

Meara and Mason stepped up beside Jake, the others of the team stopping a few yards behind him.

"I believe the answers we're looking for are in there," said Mason.

"Uh, huh," droned Meara. "And you have the questions all ready?"

"I have a general idea."

"Really?" Meara frowned.

"I do," Mason stated flatly. Then, "Our journey has certainly raised additional concerns, but my overall apprehensions remain the same, and so my questions."

He seemed quite satisfied with his response.

"Uh, huh," Meara droned again.

Jake had heard it all before and chose to stay out of the back and forth bantering. He looked up at the gray sky, then nodded to a wide spot in the road just ahead.

"We'll camp there tonight," he stated, then looked again to the wall of trees. "It'll be dark soon."

"Right," said Meara. "As good a place as any."

"We'll head in come morning."

Mason only grumbled assent, took a few steps out ahead of them and stood looking to the trees. Betty and Carlo moved off the road to begin setting up camp.

"Waddya think, sir?" asked Meara.

"About?"

"Mason," said Meara, looking curiously at Mason, standing silent, unmoving, studying the forest they would be going into in the morning.

"I've learned not to dismiss his observations out of hand," said Jake. He sensed Meara's raised brow and grinned. "I know. I sound like Sheriff Smith."

"Yes sir," Meara said softly. "Still, whether or not he knows the questions to ask, we could do with some answers."

Up ahead, Mason took another slow step forward, continued to study the increasing shadows moving about in the trees.

§

Meara set her plate aside, stood and walked up onto the road. She walked over to Jake, who was standing with his plate in hand, finishing his meal. He said nothing, and for a long minute neither did Meara.

"It sure is quiet," she said at last.

"I'd be surprised if it wasn't."

"Guess that's so."

They fell quiet again, another long minute passed.

Meara looked about them, curious, thinking...

"The outside," she said, quietly so as not to disturb the evening. "What's it like?"

"Outside?"

Meara indicated the distant horizon, as if there was something beyond. "The world out there, where you grew up."

"Ah." Jake considered, held out his empty plate and shook off what crumbs might remain. "Crowded big cities, towns small and big, sprawling corporate farms; lakes and mountains; oceans. Lots of oceans."

"Did you like it there?"

Jake shrugged. "Some, I guess. A lot of it was too crowded, a lot of it too noisy."

"That sounds... not so good."

"Some of it wasn't. But a lot of it was nice; really nice."

"Oh," said Meara, not totally convinced. "What about your family?"

"There was just my mom."

"Were you close?" Meara was close to her own mother.

"I guess so." Jake gave a shrug. "Being just her and me, you know. It was just kind of how it was."

"Yeah, I can see that." Meara appeared a bit uncomfortable, then. "So now, you know, not being able to home again."

"Serpent's Keep is home now," said Jake. He took a moment, considered. "Mom passed away a couple of years ago."

"I'm sorry."

"Yeah, well," Jake gave another shrug. "Like I said. Serpent's Keep is home now."

"And you have family here. Your uncle." She wondered then, "Master Quigley... your mom's brother?"

"No," said Jake. "I don't think so."

Meara waited for more, but Jake didn't offer any more.

"So..." Meara pointed, indicated the road ahead of them. "I think I'll take a walk."

Captain walked across the Farm's main compound to the larger of the barns. He worked his way around to the side of the barn and down to a side door set near the middle of the building. He glanced about before entering. All was calm and quiet; it was late evening, the sky was clear, gray and quickly growing darker.

The farm manager's office was sparsely furnished with a desk and chair, several guest chairs; one short file cabinet and a small table were against the back wall. A window near the door let in the fading evening light.

Captain stepped around the desk to the counter and poured himself a cup of coffee. He settled then into the desk chair, leaned back and took a deep swallow of the hot coffee.

He looked about the room, scowled.

This just wasn't him; an interesting diversion perhaps, but nothing more than that. He looked forward to handing this off to Janice and moving on. He would honor his obligations to the strange, crazy lady and provide support as agreed to, but Captain was ready to return home. Supplies had already been loaded onto several wagons in anticipation of his departure.

The door to the office opened and one of Captain's lieutenants came into the room. He stood at the desk and waited to be acknowledged.

Captain took another sip from his coffee, looked over the cup at the young man.

"What is it?" he asked.

"We have word from Serpent's Keep, Captain," he stated. "The assault did not go well."

Captain stared down at his coffee, leaned forward and set the cup onto the desk. He smirked, leaned back in his chair and rested his hands on his belly, intertwined his fingers.

"I expected nothing else," he said. His expression grew dark. "Did we lose many of our own?"

"Uncertain, Captain, but I do not believe so. A number are being held captive, many have withdrawn. We should have more information soon."

"Very well. Any news of our partner in crime?"

"The Rhetani woman? Not as yet, sir."

There was a knock at the door. It opened and a middle-aged woman took one short step into the room.

"You should come outside, Cap'n," she said. "Something ya' need to see."

She waited until she saw Captain lean forward and stand, then turned about and left the office. Captain and his lieutenant followed her outside.

Standing then in the center of the compound, the woman to his left and his lieutenant on his right, Captain took a long swallow of his coffee and looked out, across to the road that bordered the farm. It was lined with dozens of villagers and robed monks. They were simply standing there, shoulder to shoulder, as if waiting for some sign to move in.

"We are way outnumbered here," said the lieutenant.

"Uh, huh," Captain stated calmly. He took a final swallow of coffee. "The supply wagons?"

"Left some time ago. They are well away, Captain."

"All right." Captain looked about the compound, to the buildings, to the surrounding fields. He absently handed his empty cup to the lieutenant. "I think we're about done here."

"Yes sir," said the lieutenant.

Captain looked to his left, raised a brow to the woman.

"Yes, Cap'n," she agreed.

Chapter Fourteen

Darkness had closed in on the rock outcropping. The robed monks were gathered around several small campfires that were set in shallow depressions on the knoll's flat crown, the firelight reflecting against the silhouettes of the huddled figures. Peter and John were sitting at one of the fires with young Ethan, the boy from Serpent's Keep.

Ethan had been sent to the temple by the sheriff of the village, the sheriff seeking the help of the monks. Finding that Master Peter was not at the sanctuary, and hearing that the temple abbot had gone north, Ethan had decided on his own to follow after him.

Peter hadn't been surprised to hear of the assaults on the Farm and the village, but he did find it curious, and a bit disconcerting, to hear that the Rhetani had sought the assistance of bandits.

What must the Rhetani have been thinking to choose to dance with the devil?

Perhaps the number of Rhetani was much less than previously suspected. Perhaps very few had been caught up in the Outland reintegration and were now forever beyond the Outland. This was possible, as little was really known of the goings-on within the walls of the temple that had been occupied by the Rhetani, and it could very well be that there was only a handful of the cult here in the Outland.

If their numbers were in fact few, and in spite of this they had decided nonetheless to conduct a simultaneous assault on both the Farm and the village, they might indeed have felt they needed the assistance of the bandits.

Peter thought it to be a desperate move. Should they succeed, what did they believe would happen next? Peter foresaw nothing good for the Rhetani, the bandits being bandits and the Rhetani being Rhetani.

Not that it would ever come to that, with or without the assistance of the monks that the village sheriff was seeking. Serpent's Keep may have appeared vulnerable from the outside, but Peter knew that to be illusion. Given the devotion of the citizenry to their home and the actual configuration of the village itself, any attempt to take and then keep Serpent's Keep would be met with tremendous obstacles.

Peter looked across the fire to Ethan. The boy was quietly munching on dried fruit and nut mix as he stared into the flames. Peter had promised him that help was on the way and he seemed reassured by that.

William, the monk that Peter had left in charge of the temple, had certainly understood the situation just as Peter knew it to be, and he would have responded just as Peter would have. Help was no doubt on its way to the village farm, may even already be there.

Which brought to mind a question, one that John had been first to voice aloud.

Time. Distance. Something wasn't right.

How had Ethan reached Peter and his companions so quickly? He hadn't traveled nearly the distance from the temple that he should have. And he hadn't been on the trail nearly long enough.

Did the strange fog have something to do with that? How could that be possible?

"If I were to hazard a guess, I would say that the Outland has not fully settled," Peter had suggested.

"The landscape is reshaping, still forming? Reforming?" asked John.

"Perhaps," said Peter. "And perhaps time itself, as well."

"If that be so," John sighed thoughtfully. "Then I suppose I should be more mindful of my evening walks from now on. Who knows where I might end up?"

Perhaps we should all be mindful of the possibility of becoming separated, thought Peter.

"For the time being, let us stay within sight of one another," he agreed. "At least until we get home."

"As to that," considered John. "The rest of our journey may prove interesting."

"Indeed."

"I don't understand," said Ethan. "I had no problem."

"And neither shall we," said Peter. "We will be home before you know it."

"And then?" asked John.

"We shall review the situation and respond accordingly." Peter turned to

Ethan. "All will be well, my young friend."

Ethan appeared comforted by that. A great weight had been lifted from his shoulders. The sheriff had given him an important task. That task, his mission, had been accomplished. He was content now to follow Master Peter's direction.

He looked forward to returning home.

An hour before dawn in Serpent's Keep, the world dark and still and quiet. The Quigley mansion was a shadowy black form along the heavily shadowed side street. Within its walls, the rooms and halls of the mansion silently waited for morning.

The kitchen was lit by one of the light fixtures that were set in the high ceiling. Tobias stood at the island counter, just finishing putting supplies into his backpack.

Mrs. Hodges, dressed in a thick, fluffy robe, handed him a brown paper bag.

"Your breakfast," she stated matter-of-factly.

"Thank you, Mrs. Hodges." He took the bag, rolled it and stuffed it into one of the side pockets of the backpack.

"Will you be meeting up with young Jacob, Master Quigley?" asked Mrs. Hodges. She was worried about Jake and Meara, though she tried not to show it.

"I don't think so. I'm afraid he's gone in one direction, while I will be heading in another altogether." Tobias closed the backpack and fastened the clasps. He lifted the backpack from the counter.

"I see," said Mrs. Hodges.

Tobias sensed her concern, then. For Mrs. Hodges, Jake would always be the little boy forever getting underfoot all those summers ago.

"He'll be fine, Mrs. Hodges," he said. "I have no doubt of that."

"I'm sure he will," she answered, perhaps too firmly. She managed a slight smile then. "Meara is watching over him."

"There. You see?" Tobias slipped a backpack strap over one shoulder. "I'm off then."

"So you are." Mrs. Hodges folded her arms across her chest.

Tobias reached out with his free hand, rested it comforting on her arm. He gave her a sympathetic smile.

"And as for me, madam; just another stroll in the wilderness." He stepped away and started toward the archway leading out of the kitchen.

Mrs. Hodges spoke softly after him, "The world isn't what it once was, Master Tobias."

"All the more reason to do a little exploring, my dear," he called back over his shoulder. He stepped through the archway, walked quietly from the back of the house and into the front foyer. The room was dimly lit.

Mr. Griffin came out of his room, tying the belt of his housecoat.

"On your way I see, sir," he said.

"I am." Tobias turned to look back at Griffin as he slipped fully into his small backpack. "You take care of things."

"It is what I do."

"That it is." Tobias turned and started again to the front door. "A sharper eye, my friend. As was recently pointed out to me, the world is not what it once was."

"Yes sir." Mr. Griffin stood unmoving, two steps from the door to his rooms. "Enjoy yourself, sir."

"Thank you, Mr. Griffin. I'm sure I will."

Jake and his traveling companions stood at the Road's end. The forest wall was up ahead, beyond a meadow of grass and wildflowers. It was just past dawn, the sun rising above the horizon on their left, spreading dawn colors across the meadow.

As inviting as this looked, it only reminded Jake once again that they were definitely no longer traveling the route from the outside world to the village, those summer bus trips he had taken as a child.

He readied to start across the meadow.

Meara placed a hand on Jake's arm. "Uh... what's that?"

Thin streams of fog began creeping out from the trees. The fog grew thicker as it gently rolled across the meadow toward Jake and the others.

"You don't see that every day," said Jake.

"It's about what I would expect, all things considered," said Meara.

"It's a sign," said Mason.

"A sign of what?" asked Meara, with more than a hint of irritation.

"We are being called," said Mason. "What we seek lay within."

"Right." Meara was growing annoyed with Mason's cryptic comments that took them nowhere they wouldn't be going in any case.

"Good to know," mumbled Jake. He took a long, deep breath. "Shall we?"

"Sure," grumbled Meara. "Why not?"

The others stepped up beside Jake and Meara, each giving a strong nod to Jake.

"All right, then," said Jake. He stepped forward, led his companions across the meadow, into the fog and into the forest.

TahLyn followed Aldwyn's assistant down one hallway and then another. Corwin was patient and yet insistent, pausing to wait for her at one turn and then another. For her part, TahLyn had never felt so uncomfortable. Passageways such as this were very oppressive to her.

Why do humans create such things?

She stepped from yet another passage and into a large foyer. There were a number of closed doors along the walls. Corwin stood before a set of large, heavy double doors, again waiting patiently for TahLyn. He turned then and pushed down on the wooden handles and pushed open the doors. He stepped through and stood to one side, allowing TahLyn to enter the room beyond.

It was a round chamber, forty feet across, with russet-brown stone walls and a domed ceiling. Several chairs and side tables were set against the wall to TahLyn's left, beside a set of French doors leading outside. Light spilled onto the chamber floor from the doors' inset windows.

Aldwyn was standing before the main feature in the room, what at first suggested to TahLyn a thin curtain of water, four feet across and seven feet tall. It hung midair in the middle of the chamber, two feet above the floor. It was half an inch thick. It shimmered and sparkled.

Aldwyn looked back at TahLyn, gave her a soft smile. He turned again, facing the portal, moved around the portal and looked back through it to TahLyn.

"A window on the universe," he said. He lifted a hand and gave a gentle wave, the portal shimmered and cleared. An image appeared… the open plain that TahLyn and her companions had traveled. The cloudless sky was a bright blue. He waved again, the image faded and a moment later a new one appeared; a forest canopy, the green spreading out as far as could be seen.

"You can travel where you wish?" asked TahLyn.

"Sadly, no. It is a viewing portal only." Aldwyn moved around the portal and approached TahLyn. Behind him, the portal again took on the appearance of a thin curtain of water.

"Friend TahLyn," he said then. "You are rested from your journey?"

"I am quite well, Guardian," said TahLyn. "Thank you for your hospitality."

"You are quite welcome," said Aldwyn. "And I do apologize for not being more attentive to my guests. Busy, busy, you know. I trust Corwin has stood well in my stead?"

TahLyn gave an acknowledging nod to Corwin, who was standing silent near the door. "He has been most courteous."

"Very good," said Aldwyn, walking to the chairs and side tables that were set against the wall near the French doors. He poured water from a decanter into a tall glass.

"Water?" he asked.

"No thank you."

"Nature's tonic." Aldwyn took a long drink and set the glass back onto the table. "So. Your quarters. Satisfactory? Please, if you need anything, do not hesitate to ask."

Individual quarters had been prepared specific to the needs of each of the three Jahai species. TahLyn's room was surprisingly similar to her dwelling back home, a high-ceilinged, dome-like room with no furniture to get in the way. Once settled in, she had visited the two Thrauhm and the Lynhaur. Their quarters likewise met their needs, the Lynhaur's quarters being similar to a shallow, cave-like room that opened to a plaza; the Thrauhm quarters were almost cavern-like, also opening to the same plaza.

"There is nothing more we could ask for, Guardian," she said. She bowed her head first to Aldwyn, then to Corwin. "We are humbled by such thoughtfulness."

"We could do nothing less, friend." Aldwyn stepped to the French doors, opened them. "Walk with me, please."

TahLyn followed the Ancient Guardian outside. It was good to be in the open once again. They followed a gravel walkway out to the middle of the garden, where Aldwyn stopped; he looked up at the clear sky, seemed momentarily lost in thought.

TahLyn was content to wait, content to stand silent under the open sky.

Aldwyn turned finally then to his guest. He asked of the Jahai village, suggesting that he knew of the purpose of TahLyn's journey, her reason for seeking the Ancient Guardian.

TahLyn took a moment to try to organize her thoughts, began then awkwardly stumbling through trying to explain that while those within the village were doing well enough, the village itself was... all alone. She quickly tried to describe what was happening to the Outland.

Aldwyn calmly held up a quieting hand.

He let TahLyn know that he knew of the situation regarding the Outland. He asked then for more information regarding the Jahai village, of its relationship with the Dark Path. He asked about Natan, leader of the Jahai.

TahLyn was warmed by the curiosity of the Ancient Guardian. It was clear to her that the Ancient Guardian was quite familiar with the Jahai, and more than that, that he cared for their wellbeing. She did her best to satisfactorily respond to all of his questions.

"Can you help us, Guardian?" she asked then. "We are alone. Threads along the Dark Path are broken. We have been unable to find a thread from the village to our fellows. Can you help us?"

Such threads no longer existed, and any threads that did remain were torn and frayed and unreliable. It was not in Aldwyn's power to repair such passageways. And while there might be someone out there who may hold the secret to redirecting or repurposing threads to connect to new gateways, such was not within Aldwyn's abilities, even if one could be repaired.

Not that all was lost to the Jahai village. While they would in all likelihood not soon see their home worlds, they need not remain alone.

It was not certain, but it may be possible for the village to come home to the Outland.

"Can you do this?" asked TahLyn.

There had been a number of issues with the reintegration of the Outland. This, Aldwyn had observed from the first. He had attempted to make minor corrections of his own, but his abilities, trained as he had been by those who had come before him, were in fact quite limited.

And then had come the isolation of the reintegrated Outland, suddenly separated from all that was *out there*, all that lay beyond. Upon witnessing this, Aldwyn found it easier to implement minor additional corrections, smoothing the rough edges of the Outland.

As yet, the Dark Path and Aldwyn's castle remained separate from the Outland, though the Outland was within reach of his viewing portal. The Jahai village, with its own tenuous connection to the Dark Path, was also beyond the Outland.

Not a part of the Outland and yet apart from the outside world, they appeared to exist in a realm all their own.

"We are in this together, friend TahLyn," said Aldwyn. "Together we will join with our fellows in the Outland, or together we will build our world here. In either case, the Jahai village is not alone."

Chapter Fifteen

Janice stepped out onto the smooth surface, a narrow ribbon of ancient roadway covered in a coarse yellow-green grass; sixty feet wide, smooth and straight, it ran east to west as far as the eye could see.

Her two companions moved up beside her.

"Isn't this the North Highway?" asked Devon, the younger of two.

That it is, Janice thought, though she said nothing.

It wasn't the same stretch of the highway that they were all familiar with, but it was definitely the North Highway.

"But... we crossed the North Highway two days ago," said Peg. She was considerably older than Devon, and a few years older than Janice. Her hair had gone salt and pepper over the last few months.

"That we did," said Janice.

"Then where is our sanctuary?" Peg looked back into the woods, from where they had come, as if she could somehow find the answer there.

They should certainly have reached their temple by now. They had noted changes to the landscape some ways back, and had continued to travel the direction that should have taken them home. Janice didn't believe they were lost, but had quickly come to realize that they were not where they thought they were, that the temple was not where it used to be, where it was supposed to be.

There were some major modifications going on, shifting in both landscape and time.

Nonetheless, Janice was still surprised to come upon the North Highway a second time.

"Interesting," she mumbled, mostly to herself.

Her traveling companions, both having escaped the village with her, appeared particularly shaken by recent events. Janice didn't know either of them very well. While they were both lifelong Rhetani, they had only recently arrived at Janice's temple.

"What do we do now?" asked Devon.

Janice looked across the roadway. The thick forest beyond was set back from the highway some thirty or forty feet. She looked then to their right and studied the ribbon of highway running to the vanishing point far in the distance. She looked to the left then. It was much the same; empty, somehow drawing her in.

She started left, began walking down the center of the North Highway.

"Janice?" Devon asked, prompting. "Where are we going?"

Janice didn't answer. She kept an easy, steady pace. Devon and Peg followed. They walked in silence for some time. It was some minutes later that Janice noticed a faint shimmering far, far ahead. She continued walking, though her pace began to slow.

Another two minutes and the horizon grayed, a misty flowing swirl; a fog was slowly creeping out from the horizon and crawling along the highway toward them.

Janice stopped, Peg stepped up beside her. Devon took an extra step ahead of them, frowning.

"What is that?" he asked.

Peg only gave a soft *hmmph* in answer.

"Yes," said Janice, looking to Peg. She moved up then and placed a hand on Devon's shoulder. "I think that's something I'd like to check out," she said.

§

A fog, faintly aglow with the midday sun, drifted across the landscape. It slowly thinned to a heavy mist, revealing a forest, a clearing, and the thin band of grass-covered highway, smooth and straight, reaching to either horizon.

Meara stepped out of the trees and started across the clearing. Mason was half a dozen steps behind Meara, Jake and the others not far behind. Reaching the highway, they stood together on the grassy-covered band of roadway.

"Curiouser and curiouser," mumbled Jake, looking west then east.

The others looked questioning at Jake.

"Yes," said Mason, agreeing with the observation while not knowing the source of the phrase. He could see, as they all could see, that this was the North Highway, though no one recognized this particular stretch of the road.

"No. No, this isn't right," said Carlo. "I don't care how twisted the Outland got, or how we ended up north when we traveled nothin' but south, we shouldn't be anywhere near the North Highway."

"Our world continues to reshape itself," said Mason. This may not have been what he had been expecting when he insisted they journey the Road in search of he knew not what, but it was certainly a good to know...

"Yes," said Jake. He looked curiously at Mason. "Are you thinking...?"

"Just a thought."

"What is it?" asked Meara. She considered a moment, and then, "Oh. I see."

"Well I don't," said Carlo.

"Neither do I," said Betty.

Meara waited for Jake or Mason to speak up. Neither did. Meara turned to Carlo and Betty.

"The question is... are these continuing changes the result of the original reintegration of the Outland, or are they guided by the unseen hand of someone else?"

She looked to Jake for confirmation. He gave a curt nod. She stepped then away from the group, again looked one direction and then the other. She half turned back to the others.

"Pick a direction," she stated.

Jake stepped forward, moving past Meara. He looked back to Meara, then Mason. Mason stepped up beside him. A silent moment passed, then both simultaneously indicated east.

She walked around them and led the way east, grumbling, "Well, that's just weird."

Corwin stepped out onto the castle's front porch and moved up beside Aldwyn. He stood silent, waiting for a sign of acknowledgement. Aldwyn was lost in thought, his gaze taking him out to the world before them. The open plain stretched out from the base of the mountain range; the Dark Path was out there somewhere.

"Our guests?" asked Alwyn at last, continuing to look outward.

"All are well," said Corwin. The Thrauhm were in fact quite comfortable, content to remain in their quarters until they were needed. The Lynhaur spent as much time on the wing as in the castle.

TahLyn, the young Bentai, did seem anxious to return home with the news that she had found Aldwyn, that they were not alone, that Aldwyn knew of their plight, that he cared and that he intended to help.

Movement caught Corwin's attention and he glanced up. The Lynhaur was circling above, hundreds of feet overhead. It glided outward, away from the mountains and out over the plain.

"Will you be able to do something for them?" asked Corwin.

"I'm working on it," said Aldwyn. In point of fact, his struggles to make even the most minor of corrections to the issues resulting from the reintegration of the Outland were limited to pushing forward those changes that had previously been initiated but were not yet fully realized.

It was not within his abilities to recreate a passage to the Jahai home worlds. The young Bentai had accepted that. But Aldwyn believed that it might be possible, that it was within his capabilities, to find a frayed passageway on the Dark Path that connects to a landing in the Outland and, while not repair it, at a minimum smooth the frays and restore some reliability.

"And by assisting the Jahai, what of our own isolation?" asked Corwin.

Aldwyn and Corwin had lived in near isolation for years, and Aldwyn was forever tied to the castle that lay at the end of the Dark Path. But there had previously existed numerous threads stretching out from the Dark

Path to all quadrants and corners of the web. This had been lost of late, and so had nearly blinded Aldwyn, leaving him with only fragmented and unreliable images of what lay out there.

A single stable thread from the Dark Path to any landing in the Outland would restore at least some sense of normalcy and go a long way to restoring Aldwyn's windows.

"I'm working on it," Aldwyn said again, now almost a whisper.

Tobias was standing on the front porch of the temple, his backpack resting at his feet. He looked up into the clear sky, then out to the trailhead of the path leading back to Serpent's Keep.

He was unsure now of the direction to take.

There were only a few monks remaining in the temple behind him. According to William, the monk that had been left in temporary charge of the sanctuary, Master Peter had gone in search of the North Temple with a small group of fellow monks, while others of the brothers had gone to the Farm to help defend against the bandits.

The temple monks had been called upon more than once over the centuries to stand against those who would do wrong, whether in defense of their own or to protect those in need. Tobias Quigley had stood with them more than once.

It would be a mistake to underestimate their abilities.

The door behind Tobias opened and William came out onto the porch. He handed Tobias a rolled scroll, a copy of the map that had been prepared for Master Peter.

"Thank you, William," said Tobias. He knelt and slipped the scroll into a side pocket of his backpack.

"Master Peter should be returning before long," said William. He had already explained that word had been sent to Peter with news of what had been happening. "You are welcome to wait."

"I thank you, but I best be off." Tobias lifted his backpack and moved to the top step.

"As you wish, sir."

"I appreciate all your help." Tobias slipped his arms through the backpack straps.

"Our pleasure," said William. "Be well, Tobias Quigley."

Tobias gave a nod in answer, started down the steps. Working his way across the clearing, he decided that he would need to stop by the Farm and ensure that all was well before continuing on to the North Temple.

He looked back once to the temple before entering the surrounding woods, gave another nod to the monk standing at the top of the steps.

§

Sheriff Smith stood in front of the Farm's main barn. He looked out beyond the compound and the cultivated fields to the dirt road running alongside the farm. A large group of monks were walking along the road, on their way back to their temple.

He looked then about the compound. The world was strangely quiet, the old normal for the farm.

The farm manager came out of the barn.

"Sheriff," said Charles. "I thought you had already started back."

"Just about." He sensed movement and looked to his right. He saw a small group of villagers and monks just disappearing between two of the buildings.

They were part of a contingent of villagers and monks that were remaining at the Farm, both to help restore things and to be there and ready should the bandits decide to return. They had been driven off, but they may have gotten a taste for fresh fruit and vegetables and decide that it was worth the cost to make another visit.

Charles looked back at what had drawn the sheriff's attention. He gave an approving nod to the work going on.

"It won't be long," he said. "We'll have things back on track."

"Of that I'm sure. Did we lose much?"

"We'll be supplementing from stores for a few months, but we'll be all right." Charles gave another nod then in the direction of the sound of hammering just coming from behind the barn. "And we're putting together a couple of new wagons.

"Let me know if you need any more help." Sheriff Smith held out his hand. Charles took it and they shook. "I'll let the folks back home know how the farm is faring."

"Tell them not to worry," said Charles.

"I'll do that." Sheriff Smith started away, toward the road.

Charles called after him. "We got off easy this time, Sheriff. Injuries and all," he said. "It could be worse next time; could be a lot worse."

The sheriff gave only a slow nod of acknowledgement, turned away and started again for the road and home.

Chapter Sixteen

Master Peter called for a brief halt, the group having been hiking steadily since their midday lunch break. He sent one of his brother monks ahead a hundred paces to stand watch, another to backtrack along their path the same distance.

The Outland forest floor they traveled was little changed since leaving the North Temple some two days earlier. The canopy overhead would let sunlight stream through and then would not. The forest was quiet but for the occasional sounds of birds in the trees, small animals scurrying about the mulchy floor. The strange fog would appear, would drift through the trees and then slowly fade.

The young man Ethan had been quiet for most of the journey. He had commented to Master Peter as an aside several times that the way they traveled appeared not to be the same as his travel out, but acknowledged that he might be mistaken.

Peter looked over now at the boy. Ethan was sitting off by himself, his back to a tree. The other brother monks were sitting together some few yards away.

John returned from a short foray through their surroundings.

"All's quiet," he said, stepping up beside Peter.

"Thank you, John."

One of the two monks sent to stand watch up ahead returned, stopping when within comfortable speaking distance.

"You might want to come have a look at this, Master Peter."

"What have you found, brother?"

"It looks like some changes in the forest going forward... I don't want to get too far ahead on my own."

That being the case, Peter called the brothers standing rear watch back and the group moved out together, the afternoon break ending a minute or two earlier than planned.

Peter began noting a change after only a few dozen yards, a thinning of the forest further ahead, a brightening of the canopy. They met the second of the monks sent ahead and continued then, Peter walking in front.

The trees stood farther apart here, the trunks were more slender and lighter in color. The canopy was ever thinner, with fewer leaves clinging to spindly branches.

Fog began to form again up ahead, drifting in and about amongst the trees. It rolled slowly across the forest floor toward the group of travelers.

And then Peter came out of the trees and stepped onto a wide band of yellow-green grass that cut across the Outland as a ribbon of roadway sixty feet wide, smooth and straight, as far as Peter could see.

The others of the group followed him out onto the roadway. The sky was clear and bright blue, the slight breeze was warm.

"I suppose we should have expected something like this," said Peter. "But I didn't."

Brother John stood in the middle of grassy road, casting his eyes to the east. "This can't be."

"Oh, but it can," said Peter.

"We shouldn't be anywhere near the North Highway," said another of the monks.

"And yet, it is so."

Ethan was standing a few yards ahead of John. He lifted a hand and pointed.

"Look," he mumbled.

There was a shifting of shadows up ahead, where the highway met the horizon. Moments later then, the shadows took on the form of the silhouettes of people walking the North Highway.

Corwin stood atop the front steps, watched as TahLyn led the two Thrauhm downslope, away from the castle, to the trailhead below and into the trail that would take them down the mountainside and eventually onto the plain beyond. For the Thrauhm Jahai, it would be a lumbering, awkward hike down the steep, winding switchback down the mountain.

The three Jahai entered the trailhead and disappeared into the trees. Corwin lifted his gaze then to the sky, looking for the Lynhaur. The winged Jahai was nowhere to be seen, was probably in the low clouds that were hovering above the plain, drifting in an unseen breeze. The shadows of the clouds were scurrying across the landscape below.

Corwin turned about and started through the doors... there was work to do. The castle wouldn't clean itself.

First though, he was to report the departure of the Jahai to Aldwyn.

He entered the dome-ceilinged viewing room. Bright daylight was splashing across the floors and walls. Aldwyn was moving in slow circles around the portal window. His movements were smooth, instinctive. He was physically present, but his mind was somewhere else, somewhere distant.

Corwin always sensed something sorcerer-like about the Ancient Guardian when he was lost in such episodes. Aldwyn tended to play down his abilities, but Corwin had witnessed near mystical accomplishments many times over the years. Understanding that science underlay Aldwyn's powers did not make them any less incredible to Corwin.

Corwin moved off to one side to wait. He watched in silence as Aldwyn continued to slowly circle the portal, the Ancient Guardian's senses, powers and energies focused completely on the portal, merging with the powers of the portal, slowly becoming one with whatever mysteries lay deep in the heart of the portal.

The Ancient Guardian was far from this room, far from this castle.

Within the window portal, swirling images faded in and out, appearing and disappearing, shadowy tableaus drifting from one setting to the next. Barren landscapes, windswept plains, rolling hills blanketed in green forest.

A group of humans gathered along a ribbon of grass-covered roadway.

The last image faded…

Corwin saw then the haunting, shadowy image of Aldwyn's silhouette through the watery curtain of the portal window.

Chapter Seventeen

There wasn't a cloud in the sky.

Meara couldn't remember the last time the sky had been so clear, so blue; weeks at least, maybe months. And warm. The day was warm. Not the slightest breeze, making the afternoon all the warmer.

The group ahead continued to approach, walking toward them along the North Highway. There were at least half a dozen of them, still too far away for Meara to note any of their features.

"Warm day," she said, giving a brief side-glance to Jake, standing beside her. The others of their party were standing behind them, shuffling apprehensively.

Jake glanced up at the sky, returned his attention to the approaching group. Their silhouettes shimmered in the heat. "I expect it'll get warmer before the day is done," he said.

"I can't remember the last time it was so warm," said Meara. "The air is so still."

Behind them, Mason took half a step nearer. "It's the whole world," he said. "The whole world is still. And quiet."

"Uh, huh," said Jake.

The approaching group drew nearer, walking at a cautious, steady pace. Meara could see now that most of them were dressed in monks' robes.

She recognized the two walking in front.

"It's Master Peter," she stated. "And John."

"So I see," said Jake. He saw then that one in the group was dressed in simple shirt and pants, a light jacket.

He thought he recognized him… a kid from Serpent's Keep.

Meara recognized him too. "Ethan is with them," she said.

Right… Ethan, thought Jake. *Kid brother of one of the women of the watch.*

"I wonder how he ended up way out here with a bunch of monks," he said.

Mason stepped up beside Jake and Meara.

"I gotta wonder what the monks are doing out here at all," he said.

"They're monks," Jake said frankly. "Monks do whatever it is that monks do."

Mason frowned at that, but then gave a nod. "Expect that's true."

"Still," Jake sighed. "Be interesting to find out if they're out here for the same reason we're out here."

"Where they're coming from," said Mason.

"And if they've been seeing what we've been seeing," agreed Meara.

"Yes," said Jake. "That too."

The evening brought no relief from the heat. The air weighed heavy, the world was as still and as silent as ever. Master Peter and Jake stood apart from the simple camp that had been established. Behind them, Meara was in quiet conversation with Brother John, with Ethan close by, having attached himself to Meara.

The other monks were gathered in two groups to one side of the campsite, while the others of Jake's team had settled in near the small campfire, Carlo heating a pot of stew over the glowing coals.

"Most interesting indeed," said Peter. "Most."

"Just plain peculiar, you ask me," said Jake.

"I no longer consider any of recent events to be peculiar." Peter grinned, shook his head. "That your journey south should deliver you here is almost to be expected these days."

"And interesting…" Jake mumbled, quiet sarcasm.

"Exactly."

Jake considered, looked then back the way they had come, forward then up the North Highway from where Peter and his group had come. He gave Peter a questioning look.

"And if we went back that way, the way we came? Or if you returned where you came from? What do you suppose we'd find?"

"Ah," Peter said thoughtfully. "Now there is an interesting mental exercise."

"Uh, huh. Interesting."

Peter and Jake turned then at Meara's approach.

"Carlo says the stew's ready," she stated.

"Excellent," said Peter. He looked over to the center of the camp. Ethan was standing near the fire, looking in their direction. "You seem to have made a friend, Meara."

"I'm a familiar face," she said matter-of-factly. "Someone from home."

"Of course," said Peter.

"An island in the storm," said Jake.

Meara clearly didn't recognize the phrase, gave a half-hearted *uh, huh,* gave a nod back toward the campfire.

"Whenever you're ready," she said, turned away and started back.

Jake looked about them, looked back along the North Highway.

"You're heading home, then?" he asked Peter. Both were concerned about the attacks that Ethan had described to Peter.

"That's the plan."

"Assuming it's still there."

"Oh, it's still there, Jacob," said Peter confidently. "You have said as much in describing your experiences. Our combined observations only confirm it."

"The reintegrated Outland is doing a bit of ongoing reshaping…"

"As best we can comprehend what we are witnessing. It is quite beyond human experience, after all."

"Right," Jake sighed. He again considered. "And since Serpent's Keep, and your temple, are both in the heart of the Outland…"

"And as we are most assuredly in the Outland…"

"Then they should be here and we should be able to get to them."

"Exactly," said Peter. He pointed south. "That way."

Jake turned his gaze in the direction that Peter indicated.

"Right," he said again, not at all confident.

"Would you care to join us on our little hike?" asked Peter, grinning.

Aldwyn wore a pallid look, his skin pale, his eyes opaque, his expression distant. His right hand was raised, his fingertips just touching the thin veil of the window portal. The watery curtain reflected against his silhouette, the silk of his long robe iridescent.

The image within the portal shimmered and wavered, waned and then coalesced. TahLyn was walking the Dark Path; her Thrauhm companions followed behind her, one behind the other. The Lynhaur was nowhere to be seen, was likely on the wing above.

They approached the gateway, a passage entrance, distinct from any milestone they may have seen en route to now. It manifested no solid form. It was rather a wavering of the atmosphere along the path. The path beyond the threshold was visible and yet indistinct.

TahLyn slowed her pace, stepped cautiously nearer and then stopped. She was drawn to the entrance, sensing that this gateway was something different.

This could be it. This could be the way.

The flying dragon appeared in the image, settling down near TahLyn. It folded its wings and stepped closer.

TahLyn looked to the Lynhaur, then back to the two Thrauhm. She gave an almost human-like half-bow of her large, heavy head and looked forward again to the threshold.

In the castle of the Ancient Guardian, in the round viewing room, Aldwyn stood before the window portal.

He slowly lowered his hand to his side.

TahLyn stood atop the ridge with her companions. The gentle slope fell away down to a thinly wooded forest of oak and alder and evergreen. Broken building spires rose up from a shallow basin just beyond the trees. Nestled in the basin was the temple ruin.

Even at this distance, TahLyn could see a number of Jahai moving about among the jagged outlines of broken walls.

The temple... thought TahLyn. *Lamal's temple...*

She turned slowly about. The wooded landscape stretched out in all directions as far as she could see.

The Outland... she thought, not yet ready to voice the words aloud. *This is the Outland.*

She turned forward again, looked across to the temple ruin.

The Lynhaur stepped awkwardly forward, stood beside her.

"Many Jahai," it said.

Both of the Thrauhm grumbled and growled agreement. "Jahai."

TahLyn saw then a winged silhouette in the distant sky, approaching from the left. It glided in and began circling about high above the temple.

"Lamal," said TahLyn, speaking aloud for the first time since their arrival.

"Lamal," agreed the Lynhaur. It worked its wings against its sides.

TahLyn looked briefly to the Lynhaur, quietly noting its eagerness.

"Go, friend," she stated. "Speak with Lamal."

"I go."

The Lynhaur stepped to one side, stepped forward and readied its wings. Leaning forward, it took several hurried steps as it spread its wings and lifted from the ground, into the air.

TahLyn watched a moment, then again looked about.

The gateway was there, several yards behind the pair of Thrauhm, little more than a disturbance in the air, the threshold a gentle shimmer of the atmosphere.

A doorway between the Dark Path and the Outland.

We are no longer alone, thought TahLyn. *The village is not alone.*

She looked over at the Thrauhm. They were obediently standing by, though barely able to contain their enthusiasm, looking to the ruin and their fellow Thrauhm.

"Soon," she said to them. "We first have a task to complete."

They shifted their weight from one foot to another.

They awaited instructions.

"Find stones, this size," she said, holding her clawed hands before her, a foot apart. She pointed then. "We must build a marker there, by the gateway."

The Thrauhm went quickly about their task. While she waited, TahLyn considered their next actions. She would need to return to the Dark Path and then on to the village as soon as possible. Natan must be told. The Jahai leader would be pleased. TahLyn had reached the end of the Dark Path. TahLyn had found the Ancient Guardian.

The Ancient Guardian was a friend to the Jahai.

Perhaps this was not a path between their village and their Jahai home worlds, but it was good news nonetheless.

The Ancient Guardian had given them a passageway between the Dark Path and the Outland, a path from the Jahai Village to Lamal's temple.

They were no longer alone.

Tobias followed the small group of monks into the clearing and started across toward the front steps of the North Temple. They stopped as another monk, coming through the front doors, descended the steps and indicated the path leading around the sanctuary's main building.

Tobias gave a silent thank you nod to his escort and followed the monk. The path led to a narrow gate opening into the garden. Stepping aside, the monk held a hand out for Tobias to enter.

Tobias found Master August kneeling before a raised garden bed, weeding. Seeing Tobias, the abbot stood and brushed the dirt from his hands.

"Ah! Hello! My dear friend Tobias!" he said. He rubbed his right hand on his robes and held it out.

"And hello to you, August," said Tobias, shaking the monk's hand. "You are looking well."

"As are you," said August. "Perhaps a bit gray about the edges."

"You are too kind."

"I am seldom accused of that, friend." August indicated the bench nearby and they sat down. "Tobias, how was your journey?"

"Uneventful," said Tobias. He glanced about. "The garden is little changed; as pleasant as ever."

"But a few seasons have passed since your last visit, Tobias." August gave a slight, knowing grin. "Though I understand that quite a bit more time has passed *out there*."

"And now we come back to my showing gray about the edges," said Tobias.

"Oh, not so gray as to reflect the passage of years that I've been advised of," said August. "And therefore such evidence would suggest to me that you've done some moving about, perhaps taken advantage of the web."

Tobias looked down at his hands, rubbed his palms and clasped his hands together.

"Quite so, friend August," he sighed. He sat back. "Quite so."

August slid back then and rested an arm on the back of the bench.

"So… we are returned to the Outland," he said matter-of-factly. "The Outland… coming together again after all these years."

"That is so. And then some."

"From what I understand, there is as yet some significant settling going on."

"That is true as well," said Tobias. "Which is causing some confusion and some frayed nerves among the populace."

Master August gave a few thoughtful nods. He brought his arm down. "Would this settling of the landscape be an ongoing part of the reintegration process? Or might there be some external influence at play here?"

"Ah... you perhaps refer to our friend Aldwyn."

"He has crossed my mind," said August. "Have you seen him recently?"

"Some time back; not since all of this." Tobias turned to look at his friend. It was as if they hadn't been apart at all, and at the same time at been apart for decades. "I take it you haven't talked with him?"

"I have not. Not since... *this*," said August, indicating the garden and the North Temple. He gave the hint of a smirk. "A bit more than a few seasons," he said.

Tobias gave a light chuckle. He leaned forward then and stood. He stepped away from the bench.

"You appear to have done well," he said.

"Well enough." August again rested an arm on the back of the bench. "You?"

Tobias thought of his answer for a long time, spoke then without looking back at his long-lost friend.

"Duties performed, responsibilities met," he said quietly. "A life well lived, with few regrets."

"And what of Janice?" asked August.

"Well… there may have been a disappointment or two along the way." Tobias looked back over his shoulder, forward again. "As I said, a few regrets."

Chapter Eighteen

Mrs. Hodges filled a small thermos with milk from the fridge; she wrapped her sandwich in wax paper. Leaving the estate, she walked across the street and through the park's wide side gate. Seeing Mr. Griffin, she walked across the park and stood across the picnic table.

"Mind if I join you?" she asked. She sat then, not waiting for him to answer.

He gave a brief welcoming nod as he continued selecting pieces from his cup of trail mix, steadily eating one after the other.

Mrs. Hodges looked about them. It was a pleasant afternoon; there were a number of people in the park.

"A lovely day," she said.

338   David R. Beshears

"Yes," said Mr. Griffin. He ate his trail mix as he watched Mrs. Hodges pour milk from her thermos, then methodically unwrap her sandwich. She meticulously smoothed out the wax paper.

They ate in silence for several minutes. Mr. Griffin picked at his trail mix. Mrs. Hodges ate her sandwich and drank her milk. The sounds of children playing drifted across the sprawling lawns of the park.

Mrs. Hodges pulled a napkin from her pocket and wiped at the corner of her mouth. She carefully folded the wax paper that had been used to wrap her sandwich, slipped it into her pocket. She took the napkin then and wiped the inside of the cup, returned the cup to the thermos.

She set the thermos aside. She looked to Mr. Griffin for a moment, then looked about the park again; she glanced up at the blue sky. The breeze was slight, the sun felt warm on her skin.

She looked again across the table at Mr. Griffin. He had finished his cup of nuts and raisins. He looked silently back at Mrs. Hodges, said nothing.

It was just another day for the staff of the Quigley Estate.

Mrs. Hodges sat up straight and placed her hands in her lap. She was growing increasingly concerned for Master Quigley and Jacob. The days and then weeks continued to pass with no word. They had been gone for than two months now, Jacob starting down the Road, Tobias heading into the Outland and who knew where.

Mr. Griffin was beginning to annoy her. She knew that he was as concerned as she was, but he persisted in feigning indifference.

They had known each other for decades, had worked together for decades. Each knew the other better than anyone knew either of them.

They were more family than family.

And then there are days...

Mrs. Hodges gave an audible sigh, frowned and then let the thought pass. Mr. Griffin was Mr. Griffin and would always be so.

Sheriff Smith entered the park through the main gate. Wanda, the Captain of the Civilian Watch, walked with him. From what Mrs. Hodges could tell, they appeared unconcerned. Theirs was a casual lunch hour walk, enjoying the pleasant day as all the others in the park. They were in quiet conversation. Mrs. Hodges noted an occasional smile and even a light laugh.

Yes, some sense of normal was returning to Serpent's Keep; this, despite what was happening in the Outland, and despite recent events; and despite the significant and quite visible increase in their defenses, both here in the village and at the Farm.

Serpent's Keep had always had the wall, the gates and the civilian watch, these since the earliest days of the village. These had always seemed enough. They had never had to deal with a serious threat. Dangers had always existed beyond the walls of course, in the Outland, but no serious threat had ever breached the walls and entered the village.

They had been shaken out of their complacency; they had survived the attacks on the village and the farm and so had taken lessons from the experiences and had applied what they learned to enhance their security.

And now, within its walls, the village of Serpent's Keep was slowly returning to normal.

For Mrs. Hodges this meant worrying about Master Quigley and young Jacob whenever they were away.

They should be home by now.

She looked again across the table to Mr. Griffin. He was looking out across the park at the children playing, at families gathered around picnic tables and at villagers strolling along the winding walkways.

He seemed to sense Mrs. Hodges' eyes upon him and turned to her. A few moments passed as he sensed her thoughts, her concerns.

"Soon, Mrs. Hodges," he stated. "I am confident they will return soon."

And then there are days... she thought again.

Jake walked with Master Peter through an unfamiliar woodland. Meara was ahead of them, walking with the monks of Peter's group, young Ethan amongst them.

The others of Jake's group followed a dozen paces behind him; Jake occasionally heard the whisperings of Mason as he struggled to explain to Carlo and Betty how what they were experiencing with the shifting of time and landscape somehow fit into his original observations and their reasons for starting down the Road.

Jake caught very little of what was being said, but what he did hear made little sense to him.

He caught then a hint of humor brush across Peter's face.

"He's not as crazy as he comes across," said Jake. He wondered why he felt the need to defend Mason to Peter.

"Of course not, Jacob," said Master Peter. "I would never presume."

"Eccentric, yes. I mean, sure..."

They fell silent again. There was only the sound of the footfalls of the three groups of travelers as they tread across the mulchy forest floor.

"He really does sense things," Jake said then. "It's uncanny, really."

"I have no doubt of that," said Peter. "I have known a few such as he in my time. Spirits with a deep, living connection to our world that exists on some level quite apart from our own, that they do not understand and could never explain. I doubt they even see it, as they have never known anything else."

"Sounds about right," said Jake, glancing back behind them as they walked. Mason and the others were some dozen paces back. Mason gave a placid nod to Jake. Uncomfortable now, Jake turned forward. "He is peculiar, though. No getting around that."

"Rather colorful, to be sure," said Peter.

They both noticed then something going on up ahead. Several of the monks had stopped, grouped together, Ethan with them. They were talking amongst themselves. Meara and one of the others were continuing ahead.

Jake and Peter continued forward, wary now. As they approached the group, they saw that Meara and the other monk, twenty feet or so further on, were talking with a tall, thin, middle-aged man, dressed in simple pants and shirt.

Peter and Jake left the group of monks and approached Meara, the monk and the stranger.

"The gentleman is concerned for our welfare," said the monk. "It would seem."

"I see," said Peter.

The stranger said nothing, took half a step back. Too many people were within reach of his safe zone.

Meara looked from Master Peter to Jacob.

"The Rhetani's temple is up ahead," she stated.

"Is that so?" Peter prompted, raising a brow to the stranger.

"So he says," said Meara.

"You're Rhetani?" Jake asked the man.

In answer, the stranger looked back over his shoulder, spoke in that direction.

"There are a number of defensive measures set out, up ahead," he said. "If you wish to visit our sanctuary, I will need to guide you through."

"Booby traps?" asked Meara.

The stranger looked back at Meara, then Jake and Peter. The others of the group were clustered together further back.

He said nothing.

"That is very thoughtful of you," said Peter. "We accept your kind offer."

"We do?" asked Meara.

Peter gave a pleasant smile, held out a hand for Meara to take the lead.

"Okay, sure," Meara grumbled. She moved up beside the stranger. The two then started away. Jake and Peter followed several steps behind them, the others some distance further back.

"Might I ask," the stranger said hesitantly to Meara, breaking the silence. "Have you seen Janice?"

"Janice?"

"Janice. The principal of our order."

"No," said Meara. No, sorry. I haven't."

"Perhaps your friends."

"No. I am sure not."

"I see," he said. A few more yards, then he nodded to their left, Meara followed his steps around some unseen trap. She looked back over her shoulder to ensure the others were following in their footsteps.

"We grow concerned for her," said the stranger. "The last word we have is of Janice departing Serpent's Keep. We have heard nothing since."

"I'm sorry," said Meara. "We've been away for some time."

"I see," the stranger said again. He led Meara around another obstacle, silently indicating that she should stay close.

They continued the rest of the way in silence.

Master Peter came out of the Rhetani temple, descended the front steps and walked to the middle of the clearing. He looked about, taking in the early evening.

While the Rhetani hadn't exactly welcomed them with open arms, they hadn't been discourteous either. It was as if the visitors had no connection to the village or the farm. They offered their guests a light meal and a number of sleeping cells for the night.

Peter had gone out of his way to show appreciation. His fellows followed his direction and similarly demonstrated their appreciation, albeit with minimal enthusiasm.

They would continue their journey the following morning.

Peter saw a figure standing motionless just beyond the treeline. The man's back was to Peter, but he recognized him as Martin, Janice's long-suffering assistant.

Peter walked the rest of the way across the clearing and into the trees. Stepping up beside Martin, the man mumbled under his breath to watch the booby trap, indicating a barely visible trip wire that Peter had somehow managed to avoid.

Martin's melancholy hung heavy in the air. Then, he had been gloomy since Peter and his companions arrival.

"We live in strange times," said Peter.

"That we do," said Martin after a long moment. "I wonder where it will lead, Master Peter. I wonder where it will take us."

"I am confident the path ahead will lead us to a future that we will all be eager to embrace," said Peter. "Though there may be an obstacle or two set before us along the way."

"Some of us may face more and greater obstacles than others."

True enough, thought Peter. *But then, that is always the way.*

"Some will no doubt create their own obstacles," he said.

"Of that I am absolutely certain," said Martin. He fell silent. He took a step forward, looked absently into the shadows that were moving about in the trees as early evening drifted into dusk. There was a soft, cool breeze.

He stuffed his hands into his jacket pockets.

Something has happened to her...

He took another short step forward.

The shadows were only shadows.

Peter moved up to again stand beside Martin. He recognized the source of Martin's disquiet; the man wore it on his sleeve for all to see.

"There could be any number of reasons that she has not yet returned, Martin," he said.

"I know," said Martin.

"Of course you do," said Peter. "You are a true and loyal friend, Martin. Janice is fortunate to have such a friend."

"We have been together a long time."

"I sense more than two walking the same path, my friend."

Martin gave a barely perceptible shrug. "Maybe so."

They were quiet then for a long time. The air grew ever cooler. Peter considered excusing himself to allow Martin his thoughts when Martin looked side-glance to Peter, again forward.

"Loyalty," he said then, quietly. "I suppose so. To now, what loyalty I may have felt in the past toward Janice has always been tied to the Rhetani cause."

"The Rhetani," Peter said coolly, giving a noncommittal nod.

"As it may," said Martin, holding up a silencing hand. He considered letting the whole matter drop, after some seconds finally spoke then so that only Peter could hear. "Over the years, you might say that my personal views have diverged somewhat from those of the Rhetani."

From what little Peter knew of the Rhetani, once enraptured by their dogma, to find one's way out of their miasma would seem to be just about impossible.

Perhaps Martin's unique circumstances had allowed him the opportunity to bear objective witness to the personal cost of fealty to the Rhetani. Peter himself had on more than one occasion been witness to the withering away of the inner being of those lost in the blind pursuit of similar dogma.

And Rhetani was all-demanding, all-consuming. Individualism was given over to absolute fealty to the name that was Rhetani. Civilization and Rhetani were one. There were no thoughts that were one's own that had not been first provided by the Rhetani. Belief was what Rhetani said it was.

Religion was the belief of the Rhetani. Civilization was the belief of the Rhetani. There was no political structure other than the Rhetani.

There was no war. There was no conflict. There was only Rhetani. And that was good. With Rhetani would come universal peace.

The Rhetani and their doctrine would spread to all worlds, across all times.

Martin shifted about and looked to Peter.

"I had not considered it loyalty as such. It simply was." Martin turned around and looked back to the sanctuary now given over to the Rhetani. "Perhaps that is the power, the mesmerism, of the Rhetani."

"And now?"

"And now…" Martin considered, tried to put his thoughts into words. "I would say that my fidelity to their cause is much diminished, Master Peter." He turned to look Peter in the eye. "To be clear, my loyalty to Janice has not."

So Martin had indeed witnessed the cost of fealty to the Rhetani; the cost to his friend Janice.

"And what of Janice's beliefs, my friend?" asked Peter. "Is not her loyalty to the cause as strong as ever?"

"Very likely," Martin said despondently.

"And so, Martin," Peter stated. "You have a dilemma."

Martin stared ahead, his focus on the spreading shadows in the forest before him. Dusk was fully upon them. Night was not far behind.

"I do not," he said.

So... thought Peter. *Martin will follow Janice wherever her path may take them, setting aside his own beliefs. How sad.*

"Dilemma avoided," he said. It was clear that Martin's fealty to Janice was as strong as hers to the Rhetani.

The withering away of the inner being.

Peter wished there was some way to reach out to this soul and bring him back; he had tried to save others in the past. He had failed.

Martin was too far down the path. He would have to find his own way.

Peter placed a comforting hand on Martin's shoulder.

"I am confident that your friend will be home soon," he said. He turned about then and walked back to the clearing, across to the front steps of the sanctuary. He took them slowly and went inside.

Tobias and August stood on the grassy band that was the North Highway; the ancient road stretched away toward the horizon. Several of August's fellow monks were walking slowly along the highway a few hundred yards further on, studying the woods along either side of the road.

It was late evening, the sun having set half an hour earlier. It would be dark soon and they needed to start thinking about getting back.

"We discovered it yesterday," said August, indicating the highway. "Newly arrived, so far as we can determine."

Tobias gave a curious side-glance to August as he watched the monks working their way along the wide, grass-covered ribbon.

"Yes," said August, responding to Tobias' raised brow. "This area has been well explored; has been visited quite recently. I can assure you that it wasn't here just a few days ago."

"Interesting," said Tobias. The evening air was cool. He stuffed his hands into the pockets of his jacket. He looked back behind them, around them. They were about an hour's easy walk from the North Temple.

"It was to be expected," said August. "Should your assumption be correct that the Outland has been seeking a complete return to its original state."

"Quite right," said Tobias. Evidence suggested that the reintegration of the Outland sectors had triggered a reset, the greater Outland attempting a return to all as it was so very long ago.

But there were also clear indications, at least to Tobias, that there was additionally an external hand at work. There were adjustments and minor tweaks being made that were beyond the scope of the ongoing Outland reintegration.

Tobias knew of only a handful of people capable of attempting these modifications.

The North Highway, however, was surely a part of the Outland's reset.

Tobias took a step forward, spoke back over his shoulder.

"It takes one back, doesn't it?" asked Tobias, looking down the ancient road.

"If this goes as I expect, the highway should go full around the Outland." said August. "And soon."

"Well, if nothing else, it should make my journey home a lot easier." He turned about walked to August and continued past. "It will be dark soon. We had better start back."

Chapter Nineteen

The vast expanse of cultivated, well-tended fields spread out and away from the dirt road that ran along the western edge of the cleared land, cut from the forests of the Outland long ago. A cluster of buildings formed a compound of sorts in the heart of the village Farm.

A wagon sat in the middle of one of the fields, a group of men and women working nearby. Other than the deliberate, unhurried activity near the wagon, the farm was eerily still. A whispering hint of voices drifted across the landscape as they worked.

A small band of travelers walked along the road, silent, with even the sound of their footfalls muffled. Jake and Meara looked weary, their steps plodding and methodical. Betty and Carlo traveled ahead of them some twenty feet further up the road. Mason followed far behind Jake and Meara, seeming to be lost in his own world, having appeared so for days.

Movement near the wagon caught Jake's attention. He looked out across the field as he continued walking.

The man he recognized as the farm manager had stepped around the wagon, stood beside it now. He waved to the travelers walking along the road, now just passing parallel to the wagon and those who were gathering and loading vegetables.

Jake lifted a hand and gave a half-hearted wave in response. They continued on. A quarter of an hour later they passed the southern-most fields of the farm, commonly referred to as the south forty.

Master Peter and the other monks were no longer traveling with them. Jake and his group had parted ways with the monks and young Ethan several days earlier. Coming upon a fork in the well-traveled trail they had been following, Peter had felt the right fork would take them back into the heart of the expanded Outland, while Jake felt the left fork would likely lead them nearer Serpent's Keep.

It was possible they were both right, so the decision had been made to split up. If nothing else, should one group reach home and not the other, folks might have an idea where to look for them.

And then there had been Mason. Mason wanted to follow the left fork.

So be it.

There had been a near visible sense of relief amongst Jake's group when they came upon the Farm. Reaching the farm meant that home was only about half a day's hike down the road.

At least... they hoped the village was there.

Those they had seen working in the fields had seem unconcerned. That had been a good sign.

In any event, they would know soon enough. The road between farm and village was very familiar to all of them.

Jake and Meara found themselves silently indicating one and then another landmark they recognized as they passed; a particularly unique stand of trees, a large stone, a fallen log.

"What's the plan, sir?" asked Meara. "Once we're home."

"I expect that depends on what we find," said Jake. "I'd really like some down time."

"How do we explain what we found?"

"There is that," Jake sighed. "I suppose we just set out the facts, don't try to explain it."

Meara glanced briefly back to Mason.

"Mason's been quiet," she said, looking forward again. "I wonder what he'll have to say."

"Maybe we'll leave the interpretation to him," said Jake.

Meara grinned at that. "Yes sir."

They walked in silence another few minutes. At one point, Jake pointed to a large, towering cluster of berry bushes that he recognized. She nodded acknowledgement, pulled a handful of berries as they passed by.

"Sir," she said then, almost tentative. "Are you serious about taking some time off?"

"Absolutely."

They traveled another dozen steps.

"Good," she said then.

"Absolutely," Jake said again. "We could all use a break."

"Yes, sir."

"Yes…" Jake said after a long moment. "Lay about the mansion, get in Mr. Griffin's way, drive Mrs. H. crazy. You know… just like old times."

"Yes, sir."

"What about you, Meara? Any plans?"

"I thought I'd help out at the market booth," she said. "I haven't spent much time with my mother lately."

"Sounds nice. Your mother will like that."

"She just has me," said Meara. "I mean, she has her friends at the market, but family, just me."

"I'm sorry I've taken so much of your time."

"Not at all, sir. I wouldn't have missed any of it."

"I appreciate that," said Jake. "I couldn't have done it without you."

They continued on for another few minutes.

"Sir?" Meara prompted.

"Yeah?"

"Do you really think we're going to have some time off?

"We can always hope," said Jake.

He saw then Betty and Carlo come to a stop up ahead. They were standing near a wide spot in the road, often used by travelers between the Farm and Serpent's Keep to take a break.

"Good idea," he said to Meara, then gave a raise of the hand. "Let's take five," he called out.

Peter stepped out onto the roof of the temple. He walked casually across to the edge, stood then with his hands clasped behind his back. He looked east, beyond the Outland to the sun climbing above the horizon.

Dawn had already come. He had missed the sunrise.

The temple had survived well enough without him, of course. He had expected nothing less. But these last mornings since his return had seemed busier, fuller than in times past, and he had yet to meet the sunrise.

Much had happened these past few months; past several years, actually.

Gone was the calm tranquility of the Outland, the unchanging landscape of the world in which the temple, Peter's temple, had existed all these years. Their universe was in flux, unsettled, shifting beneath their feet. Even the passage of time itself, it would seem, was uncertain.

And so what of the future?

The temples were coming together in a loose association, forming a guild of sorts, though their role in the final design of the Outland was not yet known.

Of course not. The nature of the Outland itself had yet to be realized; nor its place in the universe beyond.

What new purpose might lay ahead for the monks in this new world, for a new purpose there must be. And what might be Master Peter's role in the new Outland?

His path, and the paths of his fellow monks, would unfold ahead of them as the landscape of the Outland was realized.

Peter could wait. He would watch, witness and be ready to serve as needed. He would help shape this world as needed, would stand ready to lead his monks into their new role as needed.

Peter gave a final appreciative look about the Outland; the forest canopy was shimmering in the early morning light.

Ah well, the day wasn't getting any younger...

He turned about then and left the rooftop.

The temple hallways were in shadow, with just half the sconces lit this early in the day. He passed a number of monks along the way; some were on their way to morning studies, others preparing to work outside in the vegetable gardens. Some had maintenance duties or kitchen detail.

He found Brother John standing at the door to the mess. John gave an acknowledging nod and indicated the dining room.

"She's having breakfast, sir."

"Thank you, John." Peter stepped through the doorway.

Janice was sitting alone at one of the tables, spooning oatmeal from a bowl. She gave no sign of having noticed Peter. No one else was in the hall.

Peter went to the buffet table and gathered a bowl of oatmeal and a spoon. He joined Janice, sat at the table opposite.

"Good morning," he said quietly.

Janice glanced across the table at Peter. She said nothing and returned to her breakfast.

A group of monks returning from one of the other temples had come across Janice the day before. She had been tired, hungry, disheveled, and though unwilling to admit it had clearly been lost. It took very little persuasion for her to accept their invitation to join them.

Master Peter had been able to get very little from her as to where she had been, what she had been doing all alone in the Outland wilderness. He gathered that she had become separated from her companions while on her way to the Rhetani temple; and though she didn't actually say so, Janice's omissions made it clear to Peter that the shifting of landscape and time had mystified and confused her.

What she wanted now was to return to the Rhetani temple; much had happened and there was much to contemplate. Peter had promised that he would take her there himself.

What place might the Rhetani have in this new world? It was obvious to Peter that it would not look anything like what Janice and her cohorts might have envisioned. This was not the universe that they had at one time sought to dominate. This Outland would not willingly accept their hand.

Peter suspected their dominion would likely never spread far beyond the confines of the temple in which they now resided.

And Janice?

Peter considered the woman sitting across the table from him, just finishing her breakfast.

Her sense of identity had been shaken; her purpose made uncertain. He saw as much in her eyes, in her manner. She had done bad things in the name of her cause, a cause that she had believed in to her very core, and it now seemed to have all been for naught.

What was left now to her?

Peter would take her home. He would watch her climb the steps and walk through the large, heavy doors. What she did once within the walls of their sanctuary was not up to him.

Whatever her history, he would bid her well.

The sun shone through the few tall, narrow windows of the dining hall.

The day was not getting any younger...

Peter focused on his bowl of oatmeal.

The Dark Path was a visible thing; a thin, winding, shadowy trail running snake-like across the barren plain that was spread aglow beneath the starry sky. A waning half moon hung in the eastern night sky, climbing slowly above the nearby range of mountains that stood silhouetted against the horizon.

Aldwyn sat before a small fire, the campsite several yards off the trail, at the base of the mountain range where mountain met plain. The thin, bare, twisting branches of the short shrubs enclosing the campsite shimmered in the firelight.

Aldwyn lifted his gaze from the fire. A lone figure was approaching, coming up the Dark Path. Distant at first, the man's pace was steady but unrushed. As he drew near, his features shifted from shadow to form, showing in the light of the fire.

He stepped off the trail and stood opposite the fire from Aldwyn. He looked up at the mountainside, the castle unseen in the dark. His gaze lowered then to where the trail of the Dark Path reached the hillside and disappeared into the trees.

He looked finally to Aldwyn.

"Aldwyn," said Tobias. "I was just on my way to see you."

"I know," said Aldwyn. He indicated that Tobias should sit.

Tobias took a moment to study the ground, then shifted his weight and eased down to his knees. He dropped back then and sat down, crossed his legs.

"All too quiet," he said. "I can hear my bones creaking."

"I'll be sure to bring chairs next time," said Aldwyn.

"I'd appreciate that." Tobias adjusted his position, got more comfortable. "August sends best wishes."

"How kind. I trust all are well."

"Quite well." Tobias again looked up at the black shadows of the mountainside. "I'm surprised to see you here, Aldwyn... this far beyond your castle walls."

"Pleasant walls they be," said Aldwyn. "But I sometimes find them confining."

Tobias understood that. He felt much the same after too many days in the mansion of the Quigley Estate.

"We share that, my friend," he said. "I have the freedom to take these occasional walks. To now, you sir have not."

"Yes, well..." Aldwyn gave a sigh, took in a long breath as he looked about them. "I'm afraid this is it for me. This is as far as my *walks*, as you say, can take me."

"Too bad. Nonetheless, you have managed to broaden your boundaries considerably."

"An unexpected benefit of my recent endeavors," said Aldwyn. "Endeavors that have made your journey here possible."

While visiting the temple ruin of the Jahai, Tobias had been surprised when a group arrived from the Jahai Village. They had in turn described the new portal forming between the Outland and the Dark Path.

And so then Tobias' journey here...

He uncrossed his legs and shifted, leaning heavily on one hand.

"Quite a lot going on," he said, looking carefully at Aldwyn. "A lot of changes."

"Very little of it is my doing, Tobias." Aldwyn clasped his hands, placed them in his lap. "I do wish I could have done more."

"I'm not sure what more need be done, friend." Tobias continued to study Aldwyn's expression. "We're about done then?"

"You mean is the Outland and our environs now what they will be?"

"And don't forget time. All settled?"

"I am not all knowing, Tobias. You know that more than anyone. But should I be called upon to say yay or nay, I would say yay. We're about done."

"I hope you're right." Tobias lifted a brow and gave something between a smile and a frown. "We have a lot of nervous folks back there, not sure what's coming, not sure what's already come."

"It'll no doubt take time for the dust to settle."

They fell silent; there was the crackle of burning branches in the campfire, the shimmering glow of coals at the base of the flames. Aldwyn lifted his head, half-turned to face the slight breeze; it felt cool on his face.

"We are apart from the outside world, Tobias."

"I've been told," said Tobias. The team sent out from Serpent's Keep had returned with news that the

Outland was alone, that there was no avenue to what they called the real world.

Hearing later that Aldwyn had created a portal from the Dark Path to the Outland had been good news to Tobias. It meant that the Jahai Village was in essence now a part of the Outland.

And of course at the opposite end of the Dark Path was Aldwyn's castle.

"It is good to have you with us, friend Aldwyn," he said.

"It is good to be here, friend Tobias."

Chapter Twenty

What had been referred to simply as the temple ruin, and that for so long had been home to Lamal, the lonely Jahai Guardian, was much changed. Much of the debris had been cleared away and dozens of rustic stone structures now lined wide walkways. The craggy shard remnants of the old outer temple walls now formed a stone palisade that encircled the Jahai settlement, of late given the informal name of Sanctuary.

This was Natan's first visit to Sanctuary, his first time away from the Jahai Village since the discovery of the Dark Path portal to the Outland. And while the village would remain the administrative capitol for the Jahai outside the Jahai home worlds,

Sanctuary was destined to become the primary colony for the Jahai. Dozens of Jahai representing a number of the dragon species already called Sanctuary home.

Natan walked the main path through the settlement, his friend and assistant Khol by his side. Many of the Jahai lined the path to watch their leader pass by. Natan gave respectful nods to them as Khol pointed out the work that had been done, the work yet to do.

They reached the center of the settlement, where more Jahai stood quietly by.

There was very little work going on during his visit.

Natan held his arms at his sides, the clawed fingers of his hands pressed firmly against his thick thighs. He turned slowly about, tried to make eye contact with each of those standing in silent respect about the compound. He lowered his large head in acknowledgment to several.

He looked then at the structures that encircled the compound. These were community buildings, serving the needs of the settlement. Beyond these were the private dwellings, built to the specific needs of the different species of Jahai. All were built using the recovered stone and beam materials of the temple ruin.

"I am quite impressed," said Natan to Khol.

Several of the Jahai standing nearby gave sharp nods of appreciation.

"They have worked very hard, Natan," said Khol.

"It shows." Natan looked then to the crowd. "You should be very proud of what you have accomplished here, my friends."

There were more sharp nods of appreciation, as well as mumblings and grumblings and grunts and growls of thank you.

Khol allowed this for another few seconds, then indicated to Natan that they should continue. He led Natan to a narrow walkway, which they followed to another path that ran along the base of one of the outer walls. They climbed a staircase of stone blocks to the top of the wall.

From here they were able to see out across the surrounding forests of the Outland. They stood quiet for some time, taking it in. The wooded landscape stretched out in all directions as far as the eye could see.

It was a landscape the Jahai would have to share. Hidden in those forests were other temples, these inhabited by humans. And out there somewhere was Serpent's Keep, home to friend Tobias Quigley and his nephew Jacob Quigley.

The Jahai had never lived in such close proximity to humans. There were relationships, to be sure, but this was different. And there had been the Great Ravine, but it had been isolated and secreted. As for the Jahai Village, it had not existed in the

Outland and required several portals to reach.

Sanctuary was to be a new experience, and where it would take them was not yet known.

Natan tilted his head to look side-glance to Khol.

It was good to have his friend again by his side. With this, at least, there had come some slight return to normal. With Khol's return had come a sense of relief; a great weight had been lifted that Natan had not realized he had been carrying.

Khol's support would help much with whatever was to come.

Looking outward again, Natan saw a shadow flickering across the treetops. Glancing up, he saw the silhouette of a Lynhaur, the flying dragon gliding high above the canopy.

"Lamal," said Khol. "He spends much of his time up there, out there. I believe he much enjoys the change in circumstance."

"Lamal has gained a new freedom, has he not? No longer bound to ancient obligations."

"That is true," said Khol. His Bentai face managed what might be considered a smirk. "I think he just likes to fly."

Sheriff Smith opened the door and came into the newspaper editor's front office. The room was small; the desk was cluttered with paper and folders, the shelves that lined the walls were filled with haphazardly stacked books, binders and files. The large front window, with *Village Gazette* stenciled on the glass, let in the only light.

There was no one in the room. Smith took a step to one side and looked through the open door set in the center of the back wall. An old printing press dominated the center of the back room. The machine looked to be well maintained, while the rest of the room was as cluttered as the front office.

Jeb Rainey was standing behind the press, wiping his hands with a cloth. The owner and editor gave a wave as he finished up whatever he was doing.

The Village Gazette was published weekly. Each issue of the sixteen page newspaper was filled with news articles, feature pieces, and just enough advertisements to keep Jeb Rainey from having to get a real job.

Sheriff Smith sat on the corner of the desk and waited. Half a minute later Jeb came into the room.

"Sorry to keep you waiting, Sheriff," he said. Jeb had a pleasant face and manner, bright inquisitive eyes. Anyone who knew Jeb, which was just about everyone in the village, knew also that there was a quick, sharp mind behind those eyes.

Smith pushed himself away from the desk as Jeb dropped himself into the chair behind the desk.

"The world keeping you busy, is it?" asked the sheriff.

"Not so as I can't get my six hours sleep a night." Jeb offered the sheriff the guest chair. "How about you? What brings you to my door?"

Smith slid the chair over to just in front of the desk and sat down.

"Things have quieted down considerable, for the most part," he said.

"So I've noticed," said Jeb. He gave a wink. "Slow news week, you know."

"Yes, of course." Sheriff Smith leaned back in the chair, placed his hands on the chair arms. "Which leads me to what brings here."

"Ah. Is that so?"

"That story in the last issue," said the sheriff. "The Mason piece."

"I hope I didn't get anything wrong, Sheriff. It was, after all, from Mason's perspective."

"Not at all. As you say, the story was written from Mason's viewpoint. And that was made clear."

"Good." Jeb slid forward, straightened and placed his forearms on the desk. "Then what can I do for you, Sheriff?"

Sheriff Smith leaned forward now, elbows on his knees.

"It was something that you reported, something he said."

"Sure…"

When Mason had gone with Jacob Quigley in search of what lay beyond the village, down the Road, he had told Sheriff Smith that there was indeed something beyond, that there was a world outside, but an outside that had replaced the outside they had known. It was important that they bear witness to what lay beyond, that the survival of those in the Outland, those in the village, might very well depend on what lay beyond.

Returning from their quest, Mason and the of the team spoke instead of a world beyond that lay forever out of their reach. The Outland was alone, a land of its own place and of its own time.

It was also an Outland brought together and again whole, of a history none in the village had known lay in their past.

Now, perhaps, if what Sheriff Smith had read in Jeb's newspaper was true, there was something more...

Mason now suggested that a reconstituted Outland had been torn from the fabric of one existence and was now in another, albeit empty void. Additionally, this had been the result of the actions that had initiated the reconstitution.

"In the article," said Smith, "Mason is saying that whatever outside universe might exist, it doesn't exist where we are."

"Yes." Jeb gave a slight, knowing smile. "Which goes just a tad beyond what he and the others said upon their return."

"Just a tad."

"And you are wondering if I had any more information, information that ended up on the cutting room floor."

"Something like that," said Smith.

"I'm afraid it's all there in the piece, Sheriff. I did try to dig deeper, but that's all he had." Jeb slid his arms off the desk, leaned back in his chair. "You know Mason. He's not one to hold anything back, so I felt confident at the time that that was all there was."

"I thought that might be the case."

"Perhaps if you talked with him yourself; you being the sheriff and all."

"I already did. As you say, he's not one to keep his thoughts to himself, and he told me no more than he told you."

"Then I'd say that's all there is."

"I suppose so. At least for now," said the sheriff. He fell silent then, frowning. Jeb Rainey studied the man's face, his expression.

"It doesn't really change anything, does it?" asked Jeb. "I mean, whatever is or isn't out there in the beyond, we are here, we're on our own, and the dust in the Outland has settled."

"Has it?" asked the sheriff.

"Settled, you mean? The monks think so. The Quigleys think so. Even those dragons, the Jahai, think so."

Ah, yes... the Jahai. They were going to take getting used to. They were something completely new to most of those in Serpent's Keep.

"Our world may be on its own," said Sheriff Smith. "But it's not the world we knew."

Jeb Rainey leaned further back in his chair.

"A more interesting world, I would argue," he said. "We have been much too complacent to now."

Jake was sitting on the top step of the Quigley Estate mansion's front steps, his elbows resting on his knees.

It was late morning, and the weather was pleasant. He could hear children playing in the park across the street.

Life in Serpent's Keep was slowly returning to normal, however isolated the village might be.

Mr. Griffin came around from the side yard, a pruning saw in hand. He was dressed in work clothes, sweat on his brow and his hair damp. He looked very much out of place.

Jake couldn't help but grin, though he quickly pushed it down.

"Mr. Griffin," he said. "How go the toils?"

A young plum tree had been damaged in a storm a week earlier. Mr. Griffin had just gotten around to pruning away the broken branches.

"It is all taken care of, Master Jacob."

"It'll live then?"

"I would think so." Mr. Griffin wasn't quite sure whether the question had been sarcasm.

"Good to hear." Jake gave a nod in the general direction of the pruning saw that Mr. Griffin was holding. "You should have let me take care of that, Griff. No problem, you know."

"The care of the grounds is part of my duties, Master Jacob."

"Sure, but—"

"If you wish a set of daily chores, young sir, I would suggest that you take the matter up with your uncle."

"Sure," said Jake, not able to push down a second grin. "Maybe I'll do that."

Mr. Griffin gave a terse nod in response, took the bottom step.

"I understand that you have taken on several community responsibilities," he said then. "I would not want you to become distracted from your new duties."

Jake had reluctantly accepted a seat on a newly formed committee, its role being to advise the village council regarding foreign relations... meaning the village's relationships with any and all Outland communities.

The seat had been offered to Jake after Tobias turned it down. Pleading time constraints, he suggested that he would not in all likelihood be available for most meetings. He subsequently agreed to serve as a consultant.

"I don't expect my committee duties to take up all that much of my time, Mr. Griffin," said Jake. He stood then. "They promised as much."

Now Mr. Griffin managed a hint of a smile. He gave only a half nod in answer.

Jake started down the steps then.

"I'm off," he said. "Having lunch at the café today."

"Is Mrs. Hodges aware that you will not be home for lunch?"

"I have so informed our dear Mrs. H." Jake started toward the gate. He stopped and looked back. "Would you care to join me, Mr. Griffin? I believe today's special is hearty vegetable stew and freshly baked bread."

Mr. Griffin had already started up the steps.

"I think not, Master Jacob. If you will excuse me, I must get cleaned up."

"I'm happy to wait," said Jake. "No rush, really."

"No," Mr. Griffin stated firmly; quite firmly in fact. "Thank you."

"Sure." Jake reached the gate and opened it. "Your loss."

"I understand." Mr. Griffin was at the front door. He looked briefly back.

There was no one at the gate. Jake was already gone.

Mr. Griffin turned away from the door and moved back to the top step. He could hear the children playing across the street, heard parents calling after them. A breeze was wafting through the trees lining the street, the aging leaves rustling.

Autumn was fast approaching.

Mr. Griffin turned back to the front door of the Quigley Mansion. He opened it and stepped inside.

He had to get cleaned up and dress.
There were duties yet to perform
this day.

~ *End*